NOTHING UP MY SLEEVE

DIANA LÓPEZ

Ⓛ Ⓑ

Little, Brown and Company

New York Boston

Copyright © 2016 by Diana López

Little, Brown and Company

Hachette Book Group
1290 Avenue of the Americas, New York, NY 10104
Visit us at lb-kids.com

Little, Brown and Company is a division of Hachette Book Group, Inc.
The Little, Brown name and logo are trademarks of Hachette Book Group, Inc.

The publisher is not responsible for websites (or their content) that are not owned by the publisher.

First Edition: April 2016

Library of Congress Cataloging-in-Publication Data

López, Diana.
    Nothing up my sleeve / by Diana López. — First edition.
        pages cm
    Summary: When best friends Dominic, Loop, and Z stumble upon the new magic shop in town, they know just how they will spend their summer vacation—mastering cool tricks so they can gain further access into the secret world of magic.
    ISBN 978-0-316-34087-8 (hardback) — ISBN 978-0-316-34089-2 (ebook)   [1. Magic tricks—Fiction.   2. Magicians—Fiction.   3. Friendship—Fiction.]   I. Title.
    PZ7.L876352No 2016
    [Fic]—dc23

2015015776

10 9 8 7 6 5 4 3 2 1

RRD-C

Printed in the United States of America

To Gene, my favorite magician

In any art or craft, the truly valuable secrets
are hard-earned.... Short cuts are an illusion.
Participation is required.

—*The Book of Secrets* by John Carney

From the beginning, we have heard
that the three rules of magic are:
Practice. Practice. Practice.

—*Magic by Design* by John Carney

conjure—
to practice the
art of magic

Z COULD ALWAYS FIND a reason to feel cursed. When he got a B on a test, he wondered about not getting an A. When he got an A, he wondered about not getting an A plus. He never got A pluses, so maybe he *was* cursed.

This was the last day of spring break, so he walked around town with his head down and his shoulders slumped. He should have been grateful for a whole week without homework, but in Z's opinion, a week wasn't long enough.

"We sit in class for months," he told his buddies Dominic

and Loop. "And all we get is one week off? I can barely catch up with the shows on the DVR."

His buddies nodded because they wanted a longer vacation, too. As best friends, Dominic, Loop, and Z had a lot in common. They even looked alike, all of them with brown hair and brown eyes. Dominic was the tallest; Loop had the spikiest hair (he bragged about spending a lot of time making his bangs stand straight up), and Z was the cutest, according to the girls at school who couldn't stop talking about his eyelashes. Apparently, his curly lashes were adorable, but Z didn't think this was a good-luck thing. His curly lashes were nothing but trouble when they caused girls to sit in the chairs he saved for his friends or to send him quizzes with questions like, "What's your favorite color?" "When's your birthday?" "Do you have a girlfriend?"

Z kicked a stone. "I can't believe we have to go back to school tomorrow."

"This vacation went by faster than a car with rockets," Dominic said.

"You mean faster than a *plane* with rockets," Loop said.

"No," argued Z. "Faster than *rockets*—just plain and simple rockets."

Loop glanced at him. "That's what we said."

"No, it's not. *My* rockets aren't attached to anything like yours are. That's why they're faster. They're the fastest of all."

Dominic and Loop nodded and said, "Okay, you win." Z smiled. He liked winning. He could forget about being cursed when he got the upper hand with his friends.

Truth was, the boys loved to compete against one another. They'd been doing this since their first day in kindergarten when the teacher took the class outside for recess, and Dominic, Loop, and Z got stuck on the sidelines after all the other kids took over the swings, seesaws, and monkey bars. That's when Dominic pointed to the far border of the playground and said, "Let's see who can reach that fence first." After a quick "get ready, get set, go," the amigos ran as fast as they could. Loop won that first race. But the next day, Dominic won the contest for who could hold his breath the longest, and a week after that, Z won for his expert tic-tac-toe skills. In fact, they had planned all sorts of contests for their spring break—a video game marathon, a Ping-Pong tournament, "pain games" like eating hot chili peppers or putting their hands over candle flames, and their own version of *Fear Factor*, which meant seeing who could handle roaches crawling under his shirt or who flinched the least during horror movies. They had intended to have a grand vacation, but Dominic had to spend time with his father in Corpus Christi, Loop got grounded for going from As to Cs on his report card, and Z had to complete a ridiculously long list of "enrichment" activities, which felt like chores, because they meant hanging out with his older brothers and sisters.

"A whole week of vacation and nothing interesting happened," he complained.

"At least it isn't cold," Loop said.

"Why would it be cold? It's March already."

"In some places, it's still winter in March. The kids up north don't have spring break until April."

"It *never* gets cold in Victoria," Dominic said. "Even when it's a *real* winter month, like December."

"Yeah," Z added. "I've never even seen snow." It was true. It only snowed two or three times every hundred years in their part of Texas.

His friends sighed because they'd never seen snow, either, and because there were so many things to complain about—like how they had to go back to school tomorrow, and how their families got on their nerves, and how they got clothes for their birthdays instead of video games.

"How many days till summer?" Loop asked as they made their way toward a shopping center on the corner of Laurent Street and Airline Road. The center had a furniture outlet, a store that sold scrubs for nurses, and gift shops called Pizazz and Rings 'N Things. The boys just meant to pass by, but then they noticed something new.

"Check this out," Loop said, pointing to a shop called Conjuring Cats. Its display window had a cape and top hat hanging from a coatrack, a black stool with a wand resting upon it, and an easel with a poster of Houdini in a straitjacket, hanging upside down over the words DEATH-DEFYING ESCAPE.

Z didn't know what the "conjuring" part of Conjuring Cats meant, so when they stepped through the door, he said, "You sell cats here?"

The lady inside laughed as if Z had asked a silly question. But how could it be a silly question? The cats were *right there*! A black one chased a ball, and a white one yawned and stretched on the counter.

"I would sell them if I could," she said, "but *she* won't let me." She pointed to a girl who had her back to them as she dusted a shelf of DVDs. She had two long braids, and she wore a hot-pink T-shirt and jeans with hearts embroidered on the back pockets. She was listening to an iPod, humming and swaying a bit. Her music must have been loud, because she hadn't turned around. Normally, Z tried to ignore girls, but this time he caught himself wondering if this one liked curly eyelashes.

After a few moments of awkward silence, he asked the lady, "So what *do* you sell?"

She waved her arm across the store. "Why don't you see for yourself?"

spectator—
a person who watches
some kind of
performance, like
a magic trick

DOMINIC

DOMINIC COULDN'T BELIEVE Z thought this was a pet store. "Conjuring" obviously meant magic, and if you weren't sure, then you could use the context clues, like they were taught to do at school. Why would there be a top hat and a Houdini poster in the window if this were a pet store? His friends sure knew how to embarrass him sometimes.

Like right now. As soon as the lady invited them to check out the store, Loop and Z ran to the aisles as fast as little kids when they hear the ice-cream truck. Okay, so Dominic liked ice cream, too, but he never ran to the truck without looking both ways first.

"Check this out," Loop said. "It's fake blood." He held up a package. "And here's fake vomit and fake poop, too."

Dominic laughed. He had to admit, it was kind of funny. What were fake blood, vomit, and poop doing in a magic store? He joined his friends as they investigated whoopee cushions, shock pens, rotten teeth, plastic roaches, and coffee mugs shaped like grenades and toilets. Then Z and Loop found a Magic 8 Ball and started asking it questions. "Do ghosts really exist?" and "If we jump into a volcano and swim through the hot lava, will we reach the center of the earth?"

The Magic 8 Ball answered both questions with "Don't count on it."

Dominic wandered off and found an aisle with tarot cards, Ouija boards, and posters of some guy named Alexander, a man in a turban who "knows all, sees all, tells all." Then he found the crystal balls and picked one up. It wasn't very large; he could hold it in one hand. He rubbed the top and whispered, "Abracadabra, alakazam, hocus pocus, presto . . . shazam. Tell me the secrets of the universe, like why the sky's blue and the rain clouds are gray." He paused a moment, searching for a word that rhymed with "gray." "Tell me when the world began," he continued, "and tell me when it'll go away." He peered into the glass orb and waited. A long minute. Then another.

"See anything?" Loop asked.

"No."

"Hey, guys," Z called from two aisles over. "Check these out!"

They joined him and found shelves full of cards. Some shelves held normal decks, the kind with cupid riding a bicycle, and some decks had cards as big as notebook paper. Others weren't full decks at all, just packets of single cards, some blank, some with the queen of hearts on both sides, and others that had a joker on one side and an ace on the other. Those were in a section called "gaff cards."

"What would you do with these?" Z wondered aloud.

Dominic usually knew the answers to questions, but this time, he was stumped.

"Let's check out the last aisle," Loop said.

It was full of top hats, capes, and magic wands. Dominic picked up one, and when he saw that the white cat had followed him, he waved the wand over it and said, "Abracadabra, alakazam, instead of a cat, you shall be a man." Nothing happened, though he tried three times. Meanwhile, Loop and Z had grabbed wands, too, but instead of casting spells, they pretended to sword fight, swinging wildly, the wands clacking as they struck each other.

That's when the girl from the DVDs stomped over. "Stop that!" she said. She had removed her earbuds, but Dominic could still hear the tinny music on her iPod. "Respect the merchandise," she commanded as she took the wands from them. "These aren't toys." She put the wands away—all except for one. She looked at it a moment, smiling to herself. Then she bounced it on her knee, and it disappeared.

"No way!" Loop said.

"Where'd it go?" asked Z.

"Can you make it come back?" Dominic wanted to know.

She rolled her eyes as if he had asked the stupidest question. Then she flicked her wrist, and the wand reappeared.

"Wow!" Z said. "So you're a real magician, huh?"

"I'm the reigning champion of the Texas Association of Magicians' teen stage contest, so, yes, I guess that makes me a real magician."

"So you did that trick and won a contest?" Z asked.

Dominic gave him a look. "That's what 'reigning champion' means." Z just rolled his eyes.

"Please," the girl said, making the word two syllables, *puh-leeze*. "This is kids' stuff." She put the wand back on the shelf. "Besides, you can't win the contest with one trick. You need a whole *routine*."

"So what was your routine?" Loop asked.

"It's too hard to explain."

"Then show us."

She sighed, all bothered. "You kids are probably too young to appreciate it."

"What do you mean?" Dominic said. "We're the same age as you."

"Please," she said, two syllables again. "Are you even in seventh grade yet?"

The boys looked down. They were in sixth grade, but they'd be in seventh grade next year.

"Ariel," the lady at the counter said, "be nice to the customers, remember?"

"They aren't customers," Ariel argued. "They aren't going to *buy* anything."

"I am," Loop said, pulling twenty bucks from his pocket. Dominic was glad Loop had a response, but he also hated when Loop showed off his money.

"You should perform your routine," the lady told the girl.

"*No*, Mom."

The lady put her hands on her hips. "Do you want your allowance or not?"

Dominic and his friends giggled, but when Ariel narrowed her eyes at them, they immediately stopped.

"Fine," she said. She did an about-face and headed to the back of the store, disappearing behind a doorway with a purple velvet curtain. Above the door was a sign reading THE VAULT.

Dominic mentally listed all the places with vaults—banks, museums, millionaires' homes, and underground headquarters for spies. Even though this doorway had a curtain instead of a twelve-inch steel door with a combination lock and retinal scanner, Dominic knew that calling it the Vault could mean only one thing—behind that curtain was a top secret place for magicians!

suspense—
curiosity about what is
going to happen next;
magicians use suspense
to keep the audience
guessing about the next
step in their routine

LOOP

LOOP COULDN'T WAIT TO see Ariel's magic routine. She probably levitated. She probably stepped behind a curtain and disappeared. No, she probably got in a box and asked someone to slice her in half. Loop would definitely volunteer for that!

"So she's your daughter?" Loop asked the lady.

"My one and only."

"Why did you name her after the mermaid from that Disney cartoon?" Z wanted to know.

Dominic elbowed him. "Just because she's named Ariel doesn't mean she's named after the movie."

"That's right," the lady said. "But we *did* name her after a famous character."

Now Z elbowed Dominic. "See? I wasn't completely wrong."

"Her full name's Miranda Ariel Garza," the lady continued, "and we named her after characters in a Shakespeare play. It's called *The Tempest*. Miranda was the king's daughter, and Ariel was his magic fairy."

Loop and his friends nodded. It made sense. Maybe Ariel didn't look like a fairy because she didn't have wings, and maybe she didn't act like a fairy because she was rude, but she had already cast a spell on them ... well ... on Loop at least. She was so pretty with her hair in *trenzas* and her eyes as brown as the best chocolate.

"Mom," she called from the back, "get the stage ready."

Mrs. Garza told the boys to follow her to the stage. Only, it wasn't a stage, just a clearing at the back of the store. Loop was disappointed. Where were the axes, swords, and knives that could cut a body in half? The single folding table was a lame setup. Mrs. Garza covered the table with a black cloth and placed a ceramic vase on it. Then she inserted a CD into a stereo against the back wall. She told the boys to sit down, but instead of comfy, stadium seats like at the movies, they had to sit on benches, the kind that go with picnic tables, all lopsided and splintered.

Loop heard Ariel from behind the curtain. "Dad, aren't you coming?" A man responded, but his words were muffled. Then Ariel said, "Well, never mind!"

She stepped out from behind the curtain. Instead of her T-shirt and jeans, she wore a ballet *folklórico* dress, bright blue with white lace on the ruffles of the blouse and skirt. Loop had seen *folklórico* dances before and knew that when the girls spun around, the top skirt lifted to show layers of colorful skirts underneath. Ariel wore a mid-calf skirt, so he could see her white, high-heeled boots. She had also tied back her braids with a silk scarf. "Give me a sec," she said, before closing her eyes. After breathing deeply a couple of times, she opened her eyes and nodded to her mom.

Mrs. Garza pushed "play" on the stereo. Loop heard classical guitar music, soft and meditative. Ariel didn't dance, but she walked gracefully to the table. She reached into the ceramic vase and pulled out a stem. She cradled it for a moment. Then she held it in front of her face and blew on it. Little by little, a red rose started to bloom. Ariel looked surprised and then pleased. She smelled it and cradled it again, the whole time her movements following the pace of the music. As she put the rose in the vase, she peeked into it and smiled. She waved her hand over the vase and, slowly, another rose emerged. She put her hands over her heart and looked up, as if thanking the sky for this gift. Once again, she waved her hand over the vase, and a third rose appeared! She took the flowers, now a bouquet, and danced with them, twirling so that her skirt lifted to show extra layers of red, like a giant flower beneath her dress. Then she put the roses back in the vase. After admiring them for a second, she untied the silk scarf that held back her braids. She shook it, so the audience could see that it was a normal scarf, just a big white square of silk. Ariel played with it the way bullfighters play with their capes. Then she made a fist with one hand and tucked the silk into it. When she opened her hand, it was gone! She made the fist again, this time pulling the silk out. It had mysteriously reappeared! Her hands went back to her heart, and her eyes back to the sky. Loop looked up, too, expecting to see an aurora borealis right there in the store. But no, all he saw was the ceiling. Ariel turned her attention to the vase again and pulled out two more silks. She gathered them, holding the corners before flipping them to reveal their undersides. All of a sudden, different colored silks started to pour out of her hands. They went from white to pink to red to purple.

Ariel twirled as she revealed them, stopping only when she had a giant flower in her hands. She held it up triumphantly at the moment the music reached a long, vibrating note. Then she put it on the table.

She was motionless for a while because the music had stopped. But Loop could tell it wasn't the end of the song, only a quiet moment. Sure enough, the music returned. Now it was fast-paced, so Ariel stomped to the beat. A few rose petals fell from her skirt. She jumped back, surprised but delighted, too. She stomped again, and more petals fell. She stomped some more, just like a real *folklórico* dancer. Then she twirled, and her skirt lifted, showing the red petticoats and even more dropping petals. They rained down. It was a total petal storm! Loop couldn't believe it. His friends were astounded, too. He could tell because their eyes were wide. *Where did all those petals come from?* Loop wondered. The music got louder and the spinning faster, and Loop got dizzy from watching. Then—just as the music reached its final and most dramatic crescendo—Ariel stomped one more time and even more petals fell from her skirt!

The music stopped, and Ariel took a bow. The boys could not contain themselves. They clapped and cheered. Loop let out a *grito* just like his uncles did when the Dallas Cowboys scored a touchdown. Usually, he didn't enjoy girlie things like flowers, but he had to admit this routine was even better than someone getting sliced in half.

"That was the craziest, awesomest thing I ever saw!" he shouted.

"No wonder you won!" Dominic said.

"Will you teach *me* to be a magician?" Z asked. Loop and Dominic wanted to learn, too.

Ariel glared at them. "Please . . . as if." Then she marched back into the Vault.

Mrs. Garza said, "Don't listen to her. You can be magicians if you want."

"How?" the boys asked.

"First you need a key for the Vault." She nodded toward the velvet curtain. "That's where the secrets to *real* magic lie. But you have to practice, too. It's all about the practice."

Loop looked at the doorway. He knew Ariel had special access. No wonder she could do all those magical things.

"How do we get a key?" Dominic asked.

"There are only two ways," Mrs. Garza said. "Either you master a trick from the store"—she nodded toward the aisles—"or you buy a hundred dollars' worth of merchandise."

The boys emptied their pockets. Dominic had $4.78, and Z had less than that, but Loop had his twenty bucks.

He always had more money than his friends, and sometimes it really bugged him because they always expected him to share.

"We're not going to spend a hundred dollars anytime soon," Dominic said, "so our only choice is to learn a trick."

"I don't have enough money to buy a trick," Z said.

Dominic glanced at the change in his hand. "I don't, either."

If Dominic's and Z's eyes could have spoken, they'd have been saying "Please!" Every time they gave Loop that look, he knew what they were asking.

"I guess we could combine our money and buy something together," he said, because what choice did he have? His buddies were broke, but they were still his friends.

"Why don't you try a beginner's kit?" Mrs. Garza suggested.

She showed them several boxes, and the boys selected one that had "a dozen spectacular tricks for beginners." It cost $24.99.

Loop realized that he didn't know the first thing about magic, but since there was nothing else to do, he figured learning a few tricks would be a fun way to pass the time. Besides, he wanted the key to the Vault and all the answers waiting behind that mysterious curtain. If Ariel could make petals appear out of nowhere, then maybe he could make something appear out of nowhere, too.

mentalism—
the art of reading
someone's mind

DOMINIC

"WAIT A MINUTE!" DOMINIC said when Loop and Z immediately grabbed a bunch of stuff from their new box of magic. They hadn't even bothered to look at the instructions. "You're going to mess up the tricks."

Loop held up a contraption called the Mafia Manicure. "This is definitely mine," he said.

Meanwhile, Z took out items and asked a dozen questions about each one.

"If you just took a minute to read...," Dominic tried to explain, but his friends ignored him. Soon all the contents of the box were on the counter, as jumbled as a heap of pick-up sticks. "We're going to lose the pieces," he complained.

After twenty minutes of squabbling, the boys divvied up the items. Dominic picked tricks that used mentalism, the art of reading someone's mind. He'd always been fascinated by telepathy and telekinesis. In fact, his favorite superhero was Professor X from *X-Men* because he could control minds. If Dominic had that power, he'd make his friends do silly things like pat their heads while quacking. He giggled just thinking about it.

Loop and Z handed Dominic the instructions for *all* the magic tricks. "Why don't you take the booklet, so you can tell us what to do," Loop said.

Dominic sighed. Every time they got a set of instructions, Loop and Z goofed off while Dominic figured things out. It didn't matter if they were learning how to play a new video game or conducting an experiment in their science class.

Finally, it was time to head home. The boys walked most of the way together, but since Dominic's apartment was closest to the shopping center, he was the first to say good-bye.

He climbed the steps to his second-story apartment and let himself in. "Mom?" he called. No answer. Then he saw a note on the coffee table: "At Lulu's." This meant his mom was next door.

Dominic and his mom had a two-bedroom apartment with a giant bathroom and walk-in closets. His apartment was just like the others in the building, except for the books all over the furniture. His mom was always getting self-help books at Hastings or the library, and since she dragged Dominic along, he'd learned to love reading, too.

His dad, on the other hand, did *not* read, except for *Sports Illustrated* or the newspaper.

Dominic shook his head thinking about how different his mom and dad were, and he wondered how they ever got married.

Then again, his parents *weren't* married anymore. They had gotten divorced when he was five. Then his dad moved to Corpus Christi and got *re*married, while Dominic and his mom stayed in Victoria. Now his mom was a single parent who worked forty hours a week as a receptionist at Crossroads Clinic. Once a month, his parents met at the halfway point between the cities—the Burger King in Refugio—where they traded him off. They might say hello to each other, but most of the time, they simply nodded from a distance. So Dominic just grabbed his duffel bag and transferred it from one trunk to another. He'd try to bridge the gap by saying "Mom told me to say hi" or "Dad told me to say hi," but his parents would just mumble something like "Tell him [or her] I said hi, too."

Sometimes he envied Loop and Z, because they got to live with *both* their parents. Loop was an only child, but he had cousins and a grandma who always visited. And Z had tons of brothers and sisters. So those guys were never bored or lonely. If Dominic had more family around, he'd have extra people to talk to. But he didn't have any cousins or siblings, at least not the full-blooded kind. He had a *half* sister on his dad's side. She was only four years old, so even if she lived next door, he probably wouldn't hang out with her. She was sweet, but she couldn't play basketball. She couldn't play anything more complicated than Candy Land and video games with ponies and fairies, which were the only things his stepmom kept in the house, saying they were age appropriate. Meanwhile, Dominic was twelve years old! They weren't age appropriate for *him*. He liked to crash race cars and shoot monsters, but his stepmom said that was too violent for Maria Elena. That was his sister's name. Not Maria *or* Elena, but Maria Elena, pronounced as one word.

He barely remembered when his parents were together. There was one portrait from Sears—his mother, his father, and his three-year-old self—but that's it. It was on his dresser next to another family portrait, one where he was posed with his dad, stepmom, and Maria Elena.

He loved his mom, and he loved his dad's side of the family, too. But every birthday and Christmas and awards assembly at school, he wanted to hang out with his *entire* family, and instead, they made him take turns. He didn't understand. Why couldn't his parents be friends?

Maybe *that's* why he wanted to learn mentalism—so he could read their minds.

vanish—
to make something
disappear

Z'S REAL NAME WAS Ezio. That's what was written on his birth certificate and report cards. But no one called him Ezio. They called him Z—not because it was easier to say, but because it was the last letter of the alphabet and he was the last kid—the last at *everything*.

He had four older sisters and two older brothers, and so far, only one sister had gotten married and moved out. The rest of his family was crammed into a tiny house, including his sister who went to Victoria College. But even a house full of people couldn't stop his cousin from coming over and spending the night, too. The cousin was two years older than Z, and when he came, he threw Z out of his own bed. Z had to sleep on the couch, which gave him a crick in the neck. And when he complained—why did *he* have to give up his bed every time?—everyone just laughed and talked about how cute he was.

Most "babies" of the family got spoiled, but not Z. He got new underwear and new shoes. That was it. His jeans and T-shirts were hand-me-downs. He got all the leftover toys and games, so they were either broken or missing parts. When serving dinner, his mother stood at the stove and made the kids line up behind her, oldest to youngest, so she had to scrape the pan when it was Z's turn, which meant he got rice that was stuck to the bottom or a tiny chicken wing. His older siblings worked at the mall or at fast-food places, but instead of saving lots of money, his whole family was broke. Who knew what his brothers and sisters spent their cash on. His parents had to feed everyone and pay a bunch of bills, so when Z asked for an allowance, he might get ten dollars, but mostly he got some weird amount like $3.19 or $5.04.

He wasn't happy about it, but he understood. It was hard to raise seven kids when you were the Floor Guy. That was the name of his dad's business, and he was really *the* Floor Guy. When you called the company, Z's mom answered, and the person who fixed your floor was his dad. They'd been doing this for years.

The house was never quiet. Everybody talked. At the same time! Stories never got finished. Z's hardly ever got started. That's why he didn't bother to say hello when he got home from Conjuring Cats. He just walked in and said, "There's a new magic shop in town, so now I'm going to be a magician." He waved his bag of magic tricks, but no one seemed to notice. His oldest sister had stopped by, and she and his mom kept talking about coupons. Margaret, Lucinda, and Corina, better known by the family as Bossy, Copycat, and Smiley—everybody had a nickname—were making fun of celebrities in the tabloids. His dad was on the phone. His brothers and cousin were arm-wrestling. His dog stood at the sliding door barking to go out. All this was happening in the main room of their house, which was the dining room and living room put together.

"I've got some new magic tricks!" he called out. He waved the bag again.

Finally, his mom noticed. "What's that, *mijo*?"

"I'm going to learn magic."

"That's wonderful. I'm so glad you are doing interesting things. It's lots better than watching TV all the time." She glanced disapprovingly at his sisters, but they didn't care.

Just then, his oldest sister interrupted. "Here's twenty percent off for Bath and Body Works."

"Even with the discount," his mom said, "it's still expensive."

Z jumped in. "I need a dollar bill. It's for my magic."

"Didn't you already go shopping?" his oldest sister asked. "What's in the bag?"

"Magic," Z explained. "But the trick I want to learn needs a dollar bill. I'm going to punch a hole in it."

"You're going to waste money?" His mom didn't seem to like the idea.

Before Z could respond, one of his brothers started shadowboxing around him. "Who's wasting money?" he asked as he faked a body shot. He was *always* punching the air and hopping around, so the family called him Boxer Boy.

Z's sisters started bickering. Bossy said, "Hey, guys. Who looks better in this dress?" She held up a magazine page showing pictures of two actresses in the same outfit. Boxer Boy headed over while Z's oldest sister held another coupon and asked his mom if she ate at Arby's, and then his dad got off the phone and announced that he was going to the shop for a few hours.

"Wait!" Z said, because he needed a dollar bill. Since his

mom was too busy with coupons, he asked his dad. "Do you have a dollar I can borrow?"

His dad checked his pockets, but they were empty. He shrugged. "Sorry, *mijo*." Then he snapped his fingers at Z's brothers. "*Ven conmigo*," he said. Z's cousin went, too, leaving Z with all the girls, but that didn't mean it was any quieter. They had moved on to gossiping about the neighbors—who was getting fat and who was in the hospital and who was buying a car they couldn't afford.

Z tried to get their attention. "Does *anyone* have a dollar I can borrow?"

Smiley looked at him. "You are so cute, Z. My friend says that if you were five years older, she'd totally date you."

"Okay, but do you have a dollar?"

She didn't answer because she was back to the gossip. Someone was pregnant and someone else got a bad haircut. And speaking about hair, Z wanted to pull his out! No one asked *him* about celebrities or coupons (not that he cared, but still). No one asked *him* to arm-wrestle or go to the shop. The dog didn't even slobber on his shoes when he got home. Every time Z walked through the door, he vanished, and that was the worst part of being cursed.

illusion—
when something
seems like
something
else

LOOP

DURING THE NEXT MONTH, Loop and his friends worked through all twelve of the "spectacular tricks for beginners." Loop was totally set to perform his trick for Mrs. Garza so he could get into the Vault, but Z kept stalling, saying that he could never practice because no one would give him a dollar. Loop *almost* handed over a buck, but he changed his mind. Seriously. How hard could it be to get a dollar? And Dominic kept practicing because he had to be perfect. He *always* had to be perfect. That's why it took him five times longer to finish stuff. It didn't matter if they were making PB&Js or taking a math test. Sure, Dominic got perfect scores lots of times, but Loop could jot down some answers and get a 70, which was still passing. And finishing early meant he could spend the rest of class sketching machines. Loop loved sketching machines—not *real* ones like washers or air conditioners, but spaceships and robots in futuristic cityscapes.

Finally, his friends said they were ready to perform their tricks, so Loop got all excited—but then he got grounded. Apparently, Cs on tests weren't good enough when you also had a bunch of zeroes from failing to turn in your homework. So the audition for the Vault had to be postponed till the end of the school year. Thankfully, he only had to wait two weeks, but in the meantime, he felt like a jailbird at home.

In addition to homework, he had chores. Today, when he came home from school, his mom said, "There's a basket of towels to fold, and then I want you to do your homework. You need to show it to me before dinner."

Loop dragged his feet as he headed to the room with the towels. His mom liked them folded in thirds. It was extra work, but he did it, putting the bath towels in one stack, the hand towels in another, and the kitchen towels in a third. He was as organized as possible, but it wasn't enough.

When his mom came to examine his work, she pointed out a few towels and said, "You have to redo these."

"Why?" he asked.

"Because you folded them with the ugly sides out." The towels had initials or flowers sewed on, so they looked nice only on one side.

"Why does it matter?" Loop asked. "They'll be in the closet. We can show the pretty side when we take them out."

Instead of answering, his mom shook out the towels, unfolding them. She said, "You rushed through this just like you rush through everything. From now on, show some pride in your work." Then she walked off.

Loop was fighting mad that his mom had accused him of rushing, even though it was true. He wanted to kick the wall or hit the table, but he couldn't afford to make his life worse. If he acted out, his mom would ground him during the summer, too, and he'd be bored to death and stir-crazy if he didn't get to hang out with Dominic and Z.

He shook his head, all frustrated. Then he finished the towels, folding them exactly the way she wanted. When he was done, he headed to his room to do his homework. His door had yellow crime scene tape crisscrossing it. It was his way of saying, "Stay out!"

Loop moved the crime scene tape and stepped in. At least

he had his own private cave. And it really was a cave, with black curtains and dark gray walls. He had cool posters of wormholes and fractals, which were these weird geometric shapes that seemed to move when you stared at them. When he turned on the black light, the posters glowed in bright oranges, pinks, and greens, and everything white turned purple. He loved staring into the posters, pretending he was in a spaceship going through a nebula like in sci-fi movies.

Loop never made his bed, and he dumped his clothes in the closet without hanging them. He didn't like to dust or sweep, either. His desk was a mess of paper. But one part of his room stayed clean—the *retablo* in the corner, a little altar his grandmother had made in honor of the Virgin Mary. It had a little statue of Mary, a rosary, and some candles. His grandma made the *retablo* when he was a baby because he was born on December twelfth, the day his church celebrated a story about La Virgen de Guadalupe. That was where he got his name—Guadalupe, or Lupe, for short. Since his first teacher couldn't speak Spanish, it sounded like "Loopy" when she said it. The kids all laughed at him, so he said, "Just call me Loop," and the name stuck.

Every month, his grandma brought fresh candles and made him pray with her. She put pillows on the floor so they could kneel. Then she did the sign of the cross and started mumbling. After a moment, she nudged Loop so he could pray, too. He didn't really understand why this ritual was so important to her, but since she never bugged him about his messy room or his grades, he went along with it.

Loop didn't like to recite prayers, so he just talked to O.G. That's what he called the little statue. "O.G." was how rappers abbreviated "original gangster," but around here, it meant "original Guadalupe." He hadn't told his grandma about the nickname, because she'd make him go to confession if she knew.

Loop lit a candle and then plopped on the bed to study. He was about to fall asleep when someone knocked on the door.

He used his horror-film voice, saying, "You may enter if you dare." Rubén, his "dad," stepped in.

Rubén said, "I'm going to the car wash. Want to come?"

"Can't. I'm grounded."

"How about watching the game later?"

By "game," he meant basketball. It was the NBA play-offs. Loop loved watching sports with Rubén, but instead he said, "I'll catch the scores tomorrow." He lifted *Ancient Civilizations of the World* and pretended to read.

Rubén got the hint. "All right, then."

As soon as he left, Loop threw his book. It landed face-down on the floor, its pages getting wrinkled. He couldn't help being angry with his "dad," not after the big lie his family had told him.

All these years, Loop had been too dumb to realize that he and Rubén didn't look alike. Rubén had curly hair; Loop's was straight. Rubén had a gigantic nose; Loop's was a normal size. Rubén had a runner's body; Loop had a wrestler's. He had never thought about these differences until he learned that Rubén wasn't actually his dad, something he had never imagined, because Rubén was in Loop's baby pictures and was dating his mom for years before she got pregnant. They even had pictures from the school dances they went to. That's how long they'd known each other.

Loop had learned the truth right before spring break. He was at his grandma's when he got in a fight after his cousin called him "Sancho's son." "Sancho" was what Tejanos called "the other man." That cousin was seriously disrespecting Loop's mom, so Loop tried to beat him up to teach him a lesson. He punched his cousin, and his cousin punched back. They got in a clench, each of them trying to take down the other. The uncles had to pull them apart. And it was a good thing, too, because Loop was about to break out some serious Muay Thai. He'd have won that fight. No way was his cousin tougher than him. As their uncles pulled them apart, Loop kept calling his cousin a liar, and his cousin kept saying, "I'm telling the truth. Just ask your parents." So Loop did. As soon as he got home, he said, "Am I Sancho's son?" His mom started crying, and Rubén told him to go to his room.

About an hour later, they came in and explained the whole thing. Back when they were dating, they had a big fight and broke up for a while. Then Loop's mom met this loser and got pregnant. Then she begged Rubén to take her back, and he did. He even proposed so they could be married when Loop was born. Rubén promised to act like a real father, and he did...except for telling this big lie all these years.

Loop hated to think about it, so he put in his earbuds and turned up the volume. He liked listening to industrial sounds—not music, just sounds like trains, clocks, sirens, revving engines, falling coins, or banging pipes. He had downloaded tracks of factory noise, too. It made him feel like he was in a machine. Sometimes he wished he *were* a machine because machines got made on purpose and *for* a purpose. They weren't mistakes, the way he was.

sleight—
the manipulation
of objects (often cards)
to create a magical
effect

LOOP

SINCE SPRING BREAK, LOOP had been counting the weeks, then days, till school ended. Now he was totally free! Okay, maybe he was on probation at home, but why spoil the illusion of complete freedom?

After perfecting the "dozen spectacular tricks for beginners," the boys had become—drumroll, please—magicians! Not like Harry Potter or Merlin, but *real-world* magicians using sleights of hand. Magic was all they talked about now, especially today as they made their way to Conjuring Cats, where they hoped, finally, to get a key to the Vault.

"We're going to blow their minds," Loop said.

Then Dominic started talking in his know-it-all voice. "The goal of performing a trick is to make the ordinary seem extraordinary; the impossible, possible; the—"

Z punched his shoulder. "Magic's for fooling people and making them laugh."

"No," Loop said. "It's for freaking them out." He lifted his shirt to show black stitches. They weren't real stitches; he'd drawn them with his mom's eyeliner pencil. In his opinion, they looked cool. That's why he drew a row of stitches somewhere on his body every day.

"I wonder what's in there," Z said about the Vault.

Loop wondered, too. "I bet there are straitjackets, chains, and guillotines. I bet there's an initiation ceremony. They tie you up, stick you in a box, and lock it from the outside. Then they wait to see if you can get out. I bet it's airtight, so you have to hurry, before you suffocate to death."

"I'm surprised you don't think there's a wormhole in there," Z said.

"That'd be cool," Loop replied. "Think about it. You step through a portal to another planet that's a lot like *our* planet, except there's magic and orange people. But they're super-nice. They like to trade their magic for things from *our* world."

"Like what?" Z asked.

"I don't know exactly. Maybe jelly beans or skateboards." The boys cracked up. Even Loop laughed at himself.

"No," said Dominic when they settled down. "I'm sure there's a sage in there."

"What's that?" Z asked.

"A wise man. There's *always* a wise man. He's usually old and decrepit, but he knows lots of stuff."

"What does 'decrepit' mean?"

"Old and hunched over and weak. Do I have to define *everything*?"

Z ignored the sarcastic comment. "Why would I want to see a half-dead guy like that?" he asked.

"Because he's wise. He's got answers," Dominic replied.

"I want to see a half-dead guy," Loop said. "I don't care if he's wise or dumb."

They walked in silence for a while, considering it. Then they arrived at Conjuring Cats.

"Hello, boys," Mrs. Garza said as they entered her shop. "Today's the big day. Are you ready?"

Loop was ready. He was going to perform the Mafia Manicure. It had taken only five minutes to learn. He hadn't even needed to read the instructions. That's how easy it was. His confidence level was at 100 percent. He was totally going to ace this magic test!

heckler—
an audience member
who harasses the
performer

DOMINIC

WHEN MRS. GARZA ASKED if they were ready, Dominic's stomach got twisted up. A few minutes ago, he was all pumped about performing, but now he just felt deflated. He couldn't explain it, since he'd practiced his trick a zillion times.

"Maybe you can go over your routines while I get the stage ready," Mrs. Garza said, and that made him even *more* nervous. Then Mrs. Garza turned to Ariel, who was writing in a little notebook. "Gather the cats," she told her.

After Ariel finished scribbling in the notebook, she

placed Spades, the black cat, and Diamonds, the white one, on the benches by the stage. They stretched out and closed their eyes for a nap. Then Ariel went into the Vault, and Dominic wondered if she was going to be in the audience, too. He had mixed feelings about that, because he wanted to show off his skills, but since she was the reigning champion, he didn't want to embarrass himself.

"Okay," Dominic whispered to his friends, "any questions about how to do the tricks?"

"It's all under control," Z said.

"Because I can explain things if I need to," Dominic went on.

"I got it, okay?" Z said. Dominic was just trying to help, so he wasn't sure why Z was getting so defensive.

"My trick's a piece of cake," Loop added, "or a piece of flesh." The boys giggled.

At that moment, a teenage couple stepped into the store. "Welcome to Conjuring Cats!" Mrs. Garza said, waving them over. "Want to see a magic show?"

They glanced at each other and shrugged. "Why not?" they said as they headed to the benches.

Mrs. Garza went to the purple curtain, poked her head through, and called Ariel. Nothing. So Mrs. Garza slipped into the Vault, and a moment later, she came out, Ariel following with her arms crossed and her whole face a giant scowl. She grabbed Diamonds to take his spot. He hardly noticed—all he did was get comfy on her lap.

With the audience seated and paying attention, Dominic, Loop, and Z went to the stage, but then they just stood there, not sure how to begin.

"One at a time," Mrs. Garza said. "Who's going first?"

Z immediately raised his hand. "I—"

"Me!" Dominic rushed to say. He didn't mean to push his friend aside, but he was going to be sick if he didn't get this over with.

"Okay, then," Mrs. Garza said, and to Loop and Z, "You two take a seat."

So now Dominic was alone on the stage. He reached into his pocket and took out a prop called a Hot Rod. It was a little stick with different colored gems. "Look at this," he said to the audience. "Both sides of the stick have the same color gems." He flipped the stick to show both sides, and sure enough, each side had the same colors. "Purple, white, blue, red, green, and yellow," he pointed out. "Now, what's your favorite color?" he asked Ariel.

She looked at Diamonds on her lap. "White, I guess."

Dominic didn't seem satisfied, so he asked the teenage boy what his favorite color was. "Black, definitely black," he said.

"But I don't have a black gem," Dominic said.

"You didn't say it had to be a color from the stick."

Dominic frowned. "Hmmm," he mumbled.

"Can you get on with it?" Ariel complained. "This is taking way too long."

"Why don't you use your psychic abilities?" Z suggested, and Dominic perked up, as if remembering something.

"You," he said, pointing to the teenage girl. "I'm sensing you like the color red."

She shrugged. "It's okay. I mean, my favorite color is really blue."

"No, it's red," Dominic said.

"I think I know what my favorite color is."

Dominic ignored her. "Let me prove it to you. Why don't you give me a number between one and six?"

She thought a moment. "Three."

"Good. Three. Now watch this." He held up the stick and pointed at the gems as he counted. "One, two, three," he said, his finger landing on blue.

Ariel shook her head as if she was watching the lamest trick in the world.

"I told you," the girl said. "I like blue."

"Wait a minute." Dominic scratched his head. "I was supposed to count from the bottom up." He repeated himself, this time starting with the gems at the bottom of the stick and landing on the red. "Abracadabra," he said, waving his hand over the stick. "I will now change *all* the gems to red." He flipped the stick again, and the gems turned red. In fact, they were now red on both sides!

"Cool," the girl said, "but my favorite color is still blue. Can you make them turn blue?"

Dominic stuttered. "Um, well, um, it only works with red."

He glanced at his friends for help, so they started clapping, Mrs. Garza joining in. After a moment, the teenage couple clapped, too, and the noise startled the cats. Diamonds meowed, and Spades opened his eyes but quickly shut them again.

"Are you kidding?" Ariel said to the whole audience. "He totally messed up."

"It's true," Mrs. Garza said to Dominic. "You had a little trouble remembering whether to count from the top or from the bottom, but your paddle move was perfectly executed. You did an excellent job of changing all the multicolored gems to red. I am more than happy to grant you a key to the Vault."

Dominic breathed a sigh of relief. He could feel the knot in his stomach starting to untie itself.

"Who's next?" Mrs. Garza asked.

Loop stood, even though Z's hand shot up again. "I guess I am," Loop said. He grabbed a little table, placed it in the center of the stage, and put a wooden block on it. The block had two holes and looked like a miniature guillotine. Once he finished setting up, Loop faced the audience. "Before I begin, I want to say that for *my* trick, viewer discretion is advised." He glanced at the teenagers, but they didn't budge. "Okay, then. Don't say I didn't warn you." He paused a moment. "For this, I need a volunteer." Z's hand went up yet again. "I need a *brave* volunteer," Loop said, making everyone laugh. He pointed to Ariel. "How about you?"

"No," she said. "I already know what you're going to do."

He smiled. "Admit it. It scares you to death, doesn't it?"

"*Bores* me to death would be more accurate."

"Ariel," her mother warned.

"Mom, he's got the prop for the Mafia Manicure. You know I've seen this a million times."

Dominic had seen it a million times, too, and it still amazed him.

"That's right!" Loop interrupted. "And when the Mafia gives you a manicure, they don't cut your nails—they cut off your whole *finger*."

"Sounds cool!" the teenage boy said. "I'd like to see you try to chop off *my* finger."

"Then step right up," Loop said.

The boy walked to the stage. First Loop showed everyone the wooden block. It had two parts, the block with a hole for the finger and a "blade" that you could slide in and out. He told the boy to put his finger through one of the holes, and then he gently pressed down the sliding blade.

"Do you feel pressure on your finger?" Loop asked.

"Yeah, dude, I do."

Then—*BAM!*—Loop punched the blade all the way through. There was a scream, not from the boy, who was laughing, but from the girl.

"Check it out," the boy said. "I can still wiggle my finger." He wiggled his finger.

"Now," Loop said, "very slowly take your finger out of the guillotine."

The teenager did as he was asked. His finger was fine.

"Oh, man," he said. "You sliced and reattached it all in the same moment."

Loop nodded, took a bow, and the audience clapped. Everyone except Ariel.

"That's *it*?" she said. "Your whole routine was, like, ten seconds."

"More important than the length of your performance," Mrs. Garza said to Loop, "was your composure. You had a heckler in the audience"—she glanced at Ariel—"but you managed to keep control and move on. That said, I have to agree that your trick could use a little more development. Next time, consider a *series* of tricks, or spend more time building the suspense. There has to be a bigger payoff for the audience."

Even though she was speaking to Loop, Dominic nodded as he made a mental note—audience control, suspense, and payoff. These were definitely important concepts. He was quickly realizing that the magic instructions told you *what* to do but not *how* to do it. For example, where were you supposed to look? How were you supposed to stand? And what were you supposed to say? He didn't have to worry about this when he practiced alone, but in a room full of people, audience control, suspense, and payoff were 90 percent of the performance.

"Yeah," Loop said. "I guess I could have drawn it out a little longer."

Mrs. Garza smiled. "Excellent! And now, I'm pleased to announce that you have earned a key to the Vault."

Loop punched the air. "Yes!"

"Okay, one more to go," Mrs. Garza said, glancing at Z.

proof—
a step in a trick that
serves to demonstrate
that magic has truly
occurred

OF COURSE THERE'S ONLY *one person left,* Z thought, *after I was rudely interrupted by both of my friends.* He couldn't believe how they pushed him aside when they knew he wanted to go first. It was bad enough being last with his family. Did he have to be last with his friends, too?

"Are you ready?" Mrs. Garza asked.

Z nodded and walked to the stage. He took a deep breath, wiped his hands on his jeans as if to dry them, took another deep breath, stretched his neck with head rolls in clockwise and then counterclockwise circles, and after *another* deep breath, he shook out his hands and . . .

"Will you hurry up?" Ariel said, impatient. "We don't have all day."

Z continued to shake his hands, and then he cleared his throat.

"Anybody have a dollar?" he asked. Nobody moved. "It's for my trick. I need a dollar." He looked at his friends, his eyes begging for help. "I forgot to ask for my allowance before I came."

"OMG!" Ariel exclaimed. "This is so ridiculous. Can I go now?"

Mrs. Garza said, "Stay right there."

Loop sighed and reached into his pocket. "All I have is a five."

"Thanks," Z whispered. "I can't believe I forgot to bring money."

Z took a pen that was tucked behind his ear. "This is a pen," he said. "And this is a five-dollar bill." He showed everyone the pen and the bill. "Mrs. Garza, just to prove that there's no monkey business, will you write your name on the bill?"

She took the pen, but when she tried to sign her name, it didn't work.

"Wait a minute," Z said, taking the pen back. He glanced

at Dominic, who used hand gestures to explain what had gone wrong. Z nodded and said, "Just a sec." He turned his back to the audience and fiddled with the pen. Then he gave it back to Mrs. Garza. "See if you can write your name now." She did, and after she returned the pen and bill, Z displayed her signature to everyone, including Diamonds and Spades, who couldn't read it because they had their eyes closed and because they were cats.

"Do you see her signature?" he asked. Everyone nodded. "Do you also see the shifty eyes of George Washington?" This time, they shook their heads. Z glanced at the bill. "I mean, do you see the shifty eyes of Abraham Lincoln?"

"This is so lame," Ariel said.

Z sighed, all frustrated. "Sorry. I never practice with a five. The most I ever have is a one-dollar bill."

"Whatever," she said.

"Well," Z went on, "I don't know if you see Lincoln's shifty eyes, but *I* sure do and they're really creeping me out. They creep me out so much that all I want to do is poke them out!" With that, he punctured the bill with the pen, leaving the pen there and making the teenage girl flinch and the boy say, "Dude, show some respect for the prez!"

Z displayed the bill again to prove that the pen had poked through and that he was truly using the bill with Mrs. Garza's signature.

Then he held up a finger. "Don't worry. It's all cool." He did another move. It wasn't very graceful, but he managed to pull out the pen, and—presto!—Abraham Lincoln was okay. There was no hole where the pen had stabbed his face, and since Mrs. Garza's initials were still there, everyone knew that this was the same five-dollar bill.

"Bravo!" cheered Mrs. Garza.

But Ariel was unimpressed. "You used the gimmick pen that comes in every beginner magic set. Big deal. I could do that same trick when I was four."

Z's shoulders slumped. Ariel was right. He had used a gimmick pen from the beginner's set. Luckily, Mrs. Garza gave Ariel's comments a positive spin. "It's true. The Pen-through-Dollar is a standard beginner's trick. But you performed it quite well, once you fixed the setup. You also added your own flare with the shifty eyes comment. I was quite startled when you stabbed Lincoln's face. And having me sign the bill ensured that you had a proof built into the trick. I do have one suggestion, and only because I want you to get better, okay?"

Z nodded.

"Make sure you come prepared," Mrs. Garza said. "Bring all the necessary supplies and complete your setup before you do the trick. It's very distracting to watch a magician getting ready. Plus, the audience figures out that he's using a gimmick. Make sense?" Z nodded. "Other than that," she went on, "I believe you are ready for the more complicated tricks that are waiting in the Vault."

"So I earned a key?" Z had to double-check, because being cursed meant he didn't get good news very often.

"You most certainly did," Mrs. Garza said.

Dominic, Loop, and Z cheered, and then they followed Mrs. Garza to the counter. Before giving them the keys, she had to help the teenage couple. The boy wanted to buy his own Mafia Manicure gimmick, and the girl wanted to buy a whoopee cushion so she could embarrass her friends. Meanwhile, Ariel grabbed her notebook and went to a corner to write again.

When the teens finally left the store, Mrs. Garza turned her attention to the boys. Instead of gold or silver keys, she took out three index cards, wrote "K-E-Y" on them, and stamped them with the official Conjuring Cats logo, a kitty with a top hat on its head and a wand in its mouth.

She handed them the cards. "You are official magicians," she said. "And with the power of magic comes a code of honor. Ready?"

They nodded.

"One, a magician never reveals his secrets to spectators. Two, a magician never repeats the same trick to the same audience. Three, a magician never uses his powers to gamble, cheat, or steal. Four, a magician gives credit where credit is due. And five, a magician never seeks revenge on the hecklers." She paused to let them absorb this. "Do you promise to uphold the magician's code of honor?"

In unison the boys said, "We promise."

She made a sweeping gesture toward the purple velvet curtain. "Wonderful! You may now enter the Vault."

reveal—
to make a secret known
to others

Z AND HIS FRIENDS walked toward the Vault. He knew there wasn't a wormhole on the other side, but he *did* expect magic to be revealed. Instead, when he pushed aside the curtain, he found a sink, refrigerator, coffeemaker, microwave, and two round tables surrounded by cafeteria chairs. Along one wall was a row of lockers and a door with a restroom sign.

"It's just a break room," Z said, unable to hide his disappointment.

Against the back wall was an L-shaped desk with a mess

of papers and a computer. A man sat there. He didn't turn around when they entered. He just said, "Come in if you must, but don't make too much noise." He hunched over his keyboard and typed, glancing at his screen now and then.

"We're here for the secrets of magic," Z announced.

The man kept his focus on the computer.

"So where are they?" Z said. "Mrs. Garza gave us the keys."

This time, the man held up his hand as if to tell them to wait. They did, but soon they got impatient again.

"Are you the sage?" Dominic tried.

The man sighed. "No. I'm the accountant." He finally turned around. Instead of a sports logo, his baseball cap had a picture of a bulldog with MEATHEAD written underneath. He also wore reading glasses that sat halfway down his nose. He had dark skin, a mustache, and a frown. "Did you spend a hundred dollars or perform a trick?"

"Performed a trick," the boys mumbled, not in exact unison, though they had tried. For some reason, Z felt like he was in detention.

"And Mrs. Garza gave you the keys?" the man asked, waving them over so they could hand him the index cards. He studied them and smiled. Then he stood up, his *panza*—stomach—hanging over his belt. He was wearing a gray T-shirt with *another* picture of a bulldog, only this one did not have any words. "Okay, then," the man said, shaking their hands. "Welcome to the Vault. All the secrets to magic are behind you."

Z turned and saw shelves full of books, binders, and videos. They were jam-packed without an inch to spare. The man walked to the kitchenette and opened the upper and lower cabinets. Inside were large plastic bins. These were a bit more organized, with labels like CUPS AND BALLS, GAFF CARDS, SILKS, THUMB TIPS, SPONGE BUNNIES, and SHELLS. But most were labeled MISCELLANEOUS.

He looked sternly at the boys. "These props are for practice. You can borrow anything in this room while you're here, but if you want to take supplies home, you will have to *buy* them. I'm running a business, not a charity. *¿Entiendes?*"

The boys nodded. The accountant seemed satisfied, so he returned to his desk and computer.

Z didn't know where to start, and neither did his friends, because they just stood there, too. *Well*, Z decided, *we can't stand around all day.* He went straight to the sponge bunnies and opened the bin. Inside were sponges shaped like rabbits. They'd been crammed so tightly that a dozen spilled out when Z opened it. The boys picked them up and examined them.

"You can barely tell they're bunnies," Dominic said. "Looks like someone used a cookie cutter to make them."

The sponge bunnies were mostly yellow, but as the boys sifted through the box, they discovered some that were green, hot pink, or red. Most were no taller than a triple-A battery, but every now and then, they found a bigger one.

"Hey," Z realized, "we've got bunny families in here."

They dumped the bunnies onto one of the tables and started to group them. That's when they noticed that there were sponge chicks, sponge hearts, and even sponge gremlins.

"What's so magical about these?" Loop asked as he carefully examined a yellow bunny. Then he took a whole bunch and squeezed his fist closed. When he let go, the bunnies popped out, quickly resuming their shape. Z tossed a few but they floated down like empty ziplock bags, making them impossible to juggle. Dominic studied them like a detective with a magnifying glass.

"Beats me," he said to answer Loop's question. "Maybe they're just toys."

The accountant cleared his throat. "They are *not* toys," he corrected. "This is a magic shop, not a toy store."

"So what's magical about them?" Dominic asked. The boys waited for a reply, but the man had his back toward them as he busily punched numbers on a calculator.

Z started to repack the bunnies, trying his best to keep the family groups together. Since there were so many, he had to squish them in order to replace the lid.

"It must be awful to be crammed in like that," Z said.

"They're sponges," Loop said. "They don't have feelings."

"But what if they did? What if they were people all crammed in a tiny box?"

"They're *not* people. They're little sponges."

"But what if they *were*?"

"They're *not*, so it's a dumb thing to worry about."

Z hated how his friends acted like all his ideas were stupid.

Dominic jumped in. "If they were people, it would be awful, but since they're sponges, it's not."

Z nodded, convinced that Dominic had taken his side, but when he saw Loop nodding, too, he realized that Dominic hadn't picked a side at all.

They returned the bin and pulled out another, and because this one was labeled SHELLS, Z thought about the beach, how he never had any fun because his brothers and sisters hogged the kites, lawn chairs, and inner tubes. But this bin had nothing to do with the beach, because instead of whelks, scallops, and sand dollars, it was filled with money!

"It's a pirate's treasure chest!" Loop said, dipping his hand and letting the coins slip through his fingers.

Z picked out a quarter. "That means it's probably cursed." He turned it over and discovered that, yes, it *was* cursed, because the coin was all hollow inside.

Dominic grabbed one, too. "You're right," he said. "This is fake money."

Z dumped the quarter back into the bin. "It's a cursed treasure chest."

Loop disagreed. "It's a pirate chest, and what do pirates do?" Z had no idea, so his friend went on. "They go into villages and steal treasure. Then they hide the treasure and create secret maps with all kinds of codes and puzzles. This must be a decoy. To find the *real* money, we need a clue. It's probably buried in here."

Z perked up. Maybe Loop was right. In any case, he could sure use some money, so he started digging through the bin.

"Maybe it's supposed to be symbolic," Dominic wondered aloud. "Maybe the hollow coins are telling us that money isn't really important—like when they say 'Money can't buy happiness.'"

"Are you crazy?" Z said. "Money can most definitely buy happiness."

"Yeah," Loop added, "and more video games, a giant TV for your bedroom, and any car you want."

Dominic shook his head. Sometimes Z wished his friend could just pretend to believe in things like hidden treasure. After a while, they gave up their search for secret clues. After they put away the shells, they decided to investigate the THUMB TIPS bin.

As soon as they opened it, Loop couldn't contain his excitement. "This is insane!" Inside were hollow, plastic thumbs. Loop slipped one on and showed his friends. "How about a thumbs-up?"

Z slipped on two and said, "I give it *two* thumbs-up."

Dominic put thumb tips on every finger. "Wish I could help"—he giggled—"but I'm all thumbs."

Loop put his hand on Dominic's head. "I got you under my thumb."

Z struck a hitchhiking pose. "Can I thumb a ride?"

Z couldn't stop laughing at their silly thumb jokes and the way they tried to outwit one another. They were about to take off their shoes and put thumb tips on their toes when Ariel walked in.

"What are you doing?" she said, as angry as the meanest, most impatient teacher in the universe. "This is a magic shop, not a toy store."

She sounded just like Z's bossy sister. He tried to apologize, but she just glared at him. Ariel was definitely a different kind of girl. She did *not* notice things like curly eyelashes.

flourish—
a fancy move meant
to attract the attention
of others; magicians
often use flourishes to
show off their ability
to handle cards

DOMINIC

DOMINIC COULDN'T BELIEVE IT. Ariel had repeated the accountant, word for word.

"Put those away," she said, marching to them and plucking the thumb tips off their hands. "You amateurs! How dare you joke about my craft? It's insulting!"

"We didn't mean to insult you," Dominic said. "We're just exploring."

"You have to admit," Loop added, "a box of cutoff thumbs is cool."

"Those are not cutoff thumbs," Ariel said. "They're thumb tips. Do you even know what they're for?"

Dominic thought they were for Halloween costumes, but he was afraid to answer. So far, he'd been more wrong than right when Ariel was around.

"Like I said—amateurs!" She walked to the SILKS bin and pulled out a red handkerchief. She made a big show of waving it in the air. Then she made a loose fist with her left hand and tucked the red silk into it. She blew on her hand, and when she opened her fist, the silk was gone. She had made it disappear! Dominic remembered how she had done the same move during her routine over a month ago.

"That is beyond cool," Loop said, "but how did you do it?"

Ariel could only shake her head. "Look here, noobs." She splayed the fingers of her left hand and then—pulled off her thumb! Of course, it wasn't her real thumb, but a thumb tip with the red silk stuffed inside.

"I get it!" Loop said, grabbing a thumb tip and a silk. He tried to do the trick himself, but when he stuffed the silk into the thumb tip, bits still poked out the edges.

"That's the sloppiest technique I've ever seen," Ariel complained. "You'll never be a magician with such awful execution."

"Ariel," the accountant warned.

Dominic had forgotten about the man because he seemed so preoccupied—he still had his back to them as he punched numbers into his calculator—but apparently, he paid attention to *everything* that happened in the Vault.

Ariel glanced at him and rolled her eyes. Then she reached in her back pocket and pulled out a deck of cards. "I'm just saying that you obviously haven't studied the art. Every beginner magician knows what a thumb tip is. You can probably buy thumb tips at Walmart. That's how passé they are."

Dominic glanced at his friends. They looked confused, probably because they didn't know what "passé" meant. He was about to explain, but then Ariel flicked the top card of the deck, making it somersault like a world-class gymnast, and then caught it—all with one hand!

"If you really want a challenge," she went on, "try hiding silks without a thumb tip." This time, as she talked, she spread the cards into a perfect fan. She did the fan again, but used only one hand. Then she squared the deck, took the top card, and made it spin on her fingertip the way a Globetrotter spins a basketball. "There are a zillion ways to hide cards or coins," she said. "You can palm them, back-palm them, sleeve them, or use a topit..." Without missing a beat, she lifted the cards and made them fall, one at a time, into her lower hand. "Of course, it takes hours and weeks, maybe even years to master the sleights. You guys have a long way to go." As she spoke, she divided the deck into three sections, making them flip over one another but somehow keeping them connected, as if their corners were joined by hinges.

Z couldn't contain himself any longer. "That is so cool! How did you do that?"

"This?" She did the fancy move again. "It's called a Sybil cut."

Z grabbed some cards and tried the move, but the whole deck slipped from his fingers. Cards flew everywhere. It was just like him, Dominic thought, to try something without thinking it through first.

"What a mess!" Ariel said as she continued to perform flawless Sybil cuts.

Z picked up the cards. "Looks like that move is too advanced. What was the other thing you did?"

"You mean this?" She made the cards fall from one hand to the other. "It's called a cascade. And this is a fan, and when I spin the card, it's called a pirouette. Don't you know anything?"

Dominic and Loop shook their heads, while Z attempted to perform a cascade. Instead of landing in his hand, the cards landed all over the floor.

"You've heard of the Buck twins, right?" Ariel said. "Everybody knows who *they* are."

"Do they live in Victoria?" Dominic asked.

"No!" She sounded offended. "They do *not* live in Victoria. Why would they live *here*? They're *famous*."

Dominic hated when he accidentally asked a stupid question.

"They are the masters of cardistry," Ariel said. "You think my flourishes are cool? Wait till you see what *they* can do with cards. Plus, they're supercute—and there's two of them! They're hand doubles for movie actors."

"What's a hand double?" Loop asked.

"Isn't it obvious?" She shook her head and rolled her eyes. "You know what a body double is, right?"

"Sure," Loop said. "They do stunts for the actors."

"So hand doubles do stunts for the actors' *hands*. You can't expect the actors to do card tricks or even simple flourishes like this." She made the top card somersault again. "It takes real skill. I'd be surprised if even half of one percent of the entire human population could do it."

"Ariel," the accountant said again. "That's enough."

"I'm only stating a fact," she replied. "Even people who know what a flourish is can't actually *do* one." With that, she started to cascade the cards again.

The accountant turned around. "Stop showing off," he said. "A true magician hides his skill and performs his routines with the most natural and invisible sleights."

"A *true* magician," she countered, "uses cardistry to fascinate the spectators and show them just how spectacular card handling can be."

Dominic smiled. He loved a good debate.

"All you're doing," the accountant said, pointing for emphasis, "is letting the audience know that you are adept at manipulating cards, which in turn robs your trick of power because they are expecting the spectacular rather than being surprised by it."

Ariel sighed. "You are so old-school, Dad."

Of course the accountant was her dad, Dominic realized. No wonder Ariel was a reigning champion. Her parents owned a magic shop!

"Today's audiences," she went on, "don't have the patience for your type of magic. They're used to David Blaine and Criss Angel."

"Yeah!" Loop admitted. "Criss Angel's my favorite. I love his geek magic."

"See?" Ariel said. "*My* generation has no idea who Eugene Burger or the Professor are."

This made the accountant stand up. "Show some respect," he warned. "Those are classic magicians."

" 'Classic' is just another way of calling someone old-fashioned, or just plain old."

"Now, that's where you're wrong. Classic acts *never* go out of style. They're timeless and beautiful."

Ariel pretended to yawn. "They're *boring*. Why do you think I'm the reigning champion of the Texas Association of Magicians' teen stage contest? If you're not moving forward, you're moving backward. If I had followed your advice, I would have come in last place. But I decided to appeal to the newer, hip generation, and I won!"

Her father's mustache twitched. "Young lady, the classics *never* go out of style," he said again, "and anyone can master magic with enough practice. It's time you realized that and learned a little humility."

"Humility is for losers, not for people who are born with talent, like me."

Mr. Garza took off his baseball cap, ran his fingers

through his hair, and put the cap back on. Then he reached into a drawer and pulled out some forms. He walked over to the boys and gave them the handouts. "Fill these out and get your parents' signatures. You fellows are officially entering this year's TAOM teen close-up contest. It's in Houston at the end of August. You have three months to get ready, so we must begin our training immediately."

"Dad!" Ariel was appalled. "They can't be in the competition."

"Sure they can," he said. "One way or another, I'm going to show you that talent is *earned*, not given." Then he turned to the boys. "Are you at least twelve years old?"

The boys nodded.

"Good. Every year, there's a magic competition with a teen division for people twelve to seventeen years old. The contest alternates between stage and close-up acts. This year is a close-up year. You have to come up with a routine that lasts between four and seven minutes. Don't worry. I can help you. I'll even give you a fifteen percent discount on all merchandise as long as you promise to wear a Conjuring Cats T-shirt to the convention. How does that sound?"

The boys could only nod.

"Wait a minute!" Ariel said, but her father held up his

hand to silence her. Then he returned to his desk and started tapping at the calculator again.

Ariel glared at the boys. "Fine!" she told them. "If you want to make fools of yourselves in front of a whole bunch of people, be my guest." Before Dominic and his friends could answer, before they could even process what had just happened, she stomped out.

stage fright—
when a performer
gets nervous about
being in front of an
audience

DOMINIC

DOMINIC WAS STUNNED. One minute, he was botching his Hot Rod routine, and the next, he was entering a magic contest. He glanced at his friends. They didn't seem stunned at all. They looked excited.

After Ariel stormed off, Mr. Garza told them to pick lockers, pointing out that the one with the giant gold star was unavailable because it belonged to Ariel. "You can keep your supplies in here," he explained. "You'll have to bring your own locks, but at this point, no one else has earned a key to the Vault." Then he gave them an overview of the contest. "You'll perform in front of a live audience that includes three judges. They are professional magicians, and they'll be judging your skills at handling magic, your creativity, and your delivery." So far, Dominic had mastered none of these. "The winner is announced during an evening stage show. It is a great honor to win, but it is an even greater honor to participate."

The boys nodded.

"But first, you must get your parents' permission." Mr. Garza went to his computer, pulled up the TAOM website, and printed copies of a brochure with all the rules. "Any questions?"

The boys couldn't think of any.

"Good," Mr. Garza said, nodding. "The training begins next week." With that, he dismissed them.

Dominic and his friends left, and as they walked through the store, Ariel glared at them again. She had totally mastered the look of an evil queen about to get her revenge. Dominic thought she might say, "Off with their heads!" but she didn't—probably because her mom was there.

"Good-bye, boys," Mrs. Garza said.

"'Bye," they called back.

When Dominic got home, he said hello to his mom and then went straight to his room, where he stood in front of the mirror with his Hot Rod. He repeated the routine. It worked every single time, even when he used blue as the favorite color.

After a while, his mom peeked in.

"What's going on?" she said. "It's time to get ready for dinner."

"I just want to get this perfect," Dominic explained as he counted one, two, three, four from the top of his Hot Rod, his finger landing on the red gem as it should.

"What happened? Your performance didn't go well?"

"It was awful."

She frowned. "Don't worry, sweetie. You can always try again. It's not easy to perform in front of an audience."

"I think I have stage fright," Dominic explained. "I can do it perfectly when no one's around."

She nodded. "I'm sure they'll let you try again so you can get that key you were talking about."

"Oh, I *did* get it. It's true that I messed up, but my paddle move was good enough for the key. I met Mr. Garza. He's the guy in the Vault."

"So he told you all the secrets?"

"Not exactly. But his room is full of resources—books, videos, magic gimmicks. He said we could borrow anything we wanted." He pointed to his dresser. "I checked out that book on mentalism. It's going to teach me how to read people's minds."

"Uh-oh," she teased. "Now you're going to know all *my* secrets."

"That's the whole point," Dominic said, and she laughed a bit. "But first, I have to get used to performing in front of people. I felt a little sick to my stomach. It was weird because I never freak out when I'm with Loop or Z."

"Everything's easy when you're with your friends."

"Yeah, I guess it is. That's why we're going to compete together."

"Compete? What do you mean?"

Instead of answering her question, Dominic grabbed the contest form and handed it to her. As she read, he told her about the convention in August, how magicians from all over the world gathered to share their techniques and routines, and how there were competitions that got judged by professionals. "They're always looking for new talent," he said. "Loop, Z, and I are going to be a team, and Mr. Garza is going to coach us. His daughter was the champion last year." His mom was still reading, making him impatient. "Can I go?" he asked. "I think it's a great opportunity."

"Wait a minute. Let me see." She studied the entry form

and started adding under her breath. "You're right," she said. "It's a great opportunity, but..."

He moaned like someone had punched him in the gut.

"Don't do that," she said.

"I can't help it," he explained. "Every time you say 'but,' bad news follows. You're about to tell me I can't go, aren't you? Just admit it."

She sighed. "Let me tell you why."

"I knew it!" Amazingly, he could already read her mind.

"Look at this," she said, showing him the form. "This is everything we need to pay in order for you to go: $150 to register for the convention *and* $50 to enter the contest, not to mention transportation to Houston, a room at the Hilton Americas—which is probably $150 to $200 per night—then food, and whatever supplies you need for your performance. It'll cost hundreds of dollars."

Dominic moaned again.

"We don't have that kind of money, sweetie. We're living paycheck—"

"To paycheck," he finished. "I know, Mom, but this is a once-in-a-lifetime opportunity. *Please.* I'm sure Dad will pay. He's got money."

"You can't go to your dad every time you want something."

"Why not?" A timer buzzed, so she rushed to the kitchen. Dominic followed. After she took a chicken from the oven, Dominic said, "What's the big deal about asking Dad for money? He *likes* to help his kids. Maria Elena gets to take tap lessons and gymnastics. For her birthday, Dad rented a pony and an inflatable castle."

"And for *your* birthday, he took you and all your friends to Laser World."

"I know. It was great! Dad loves to do fun things."

His mom didn't answer. She grabbed a catalog from the bar that separated the kitchen from the living room and tore out a page. "I would love to have fun, too," she said as she folded the page in half and then in half again. "But some of us have to work."

"Dad works, too."

Instead of responding, his mother kept folding the paper into smaller and smaller squares.

"I'm going to ask him about the contest when he picks me up for my summer visit," Dominic said.

"Of course you are," his mother replied. Now the paper was as small as a bottle cap. She put it in her pocket and headed to her room. "I've got a headache," she said before closing the door. "Go ahead and serve yourself. And put away the leftovers when you're done."

She always got headaches when Dominic talked about his father, and she always went to her room and closed the door. Dominic glanced at the bathroom, where the medicine cabinet was. *She'd feel better*, he thought, *if she'd take a Tylenol first.*

Bill Switch—
a trick that allows a
magician to take a low-
denomination bill and
transform it into a higher
denomination

Z FELT LIKE HE couldn't do anything right. When he had tried Ariel's moves, the cards fell all over the floor. But the worst part was messing up his routine—more proof that he was cursed. No wonder he'd forgotten to take a dollar for his trick and to set up the gimmick pen. Sure, he did okay in the end and got to see what was in the Vault, and sure, it had lots of cool stuff. But he knew Mrs. Garza gave him the key to be nice, not because she thought he deserved it. What did Ariel say? That she could do his trick when she was four? So he was as good as a four-year-old, huh? He bet she was keeping score in that little notebook of hers. He bet she had a secret point system and ranked him last. It was the only thing that made sense.

When he got home, the house was quiet for once. His dad sat at the table with a sudoku puzzle, while his mom did a crossword. They always did brain teasers when the house was empty. It was the only time they could think.

"Where is everybody?" Z asked.

His mom said, "Working or out with friends."

Z joined his parents at the table. "Want to do a word search?" his dad asked, pushing a booklet toward him.

"No," Z said. "I'm kinda tired. Today was my big performance at the magic shop."

He waited for his parents to ask a follow-up question, but they were too focused on their puzzles. His dad counted to nine under his breath as he tapped squares on the paper, and his mom kept mumbling, "A six-letter word that begins with 'w.' "

Z elaborated anyway. "So I did my Pen-through-Dollar trick. I messed up, but Dominic and Loop messed up, too. I kinda messed up more than they did, but I still got a key to the Vault."

"Mm-hmm," his parents said in unison.

Z knew they weren't paying attention, so he decided to test them. "And then I floated in the air for thirty seconds." He waited, but they didn't respond. "No strings attached," he added.

"That's nice," his mom said.

No one else was in the room, not even the dog. For once, he had his parents all to himself, but instead of listening to him, they stared at their puzzles.

"You didn't hear a word I said!"

His mom and dad looked up.

"Watch your tone," his father warned.

"But I'm talking, and you're not listening. You *never* listen to me!"

His parents glanced at each other, and then they put down their pencils. "We're sorry," his mother said. "We were just enjoying a quiet moment. We didn't mean to ignore you."

"Talk to us," his dad said. "What's on your mind, *mijo*?"

"Okay," Z began. "I've got an entry form for a magic competition." He pushed it toward them. "I really want to go."

"This is wonderful," his mother said. "Everybody needs an interest—like my crossword puzzles and your brother's boxing."

"And my floors," his dad added, since he knew every-thing about floors.

"So can I go?" Z asked. "Dominic and Loop will be there, too."

His mother studied the form. "It looks expensive," she said, handing it to his father. He glanced at it and handed it back to Z without reading a single word!

"Go put it on my desk," his father said. "We'll look at it later."

"But can I go?" Z asked again.

His mother reached across the table and squeezed his hand. "For something like this," she explained, "your father and I have to talk. There's a lot to consider before we give you permission."

Z knew this was code for "we don't have the money," but since the competition wasn't until the end of the sum-mer, maybe his parents could find a way to save enough. He thought about the Bill Switch, where a magician took a one-dollar bill, folded it up, and then *unfolded* it to reveal a ten- or twenty-dollar bill instead. So maybe it *was* possible to take a little bit of money and turn it into a lot.

He decided to hope for the best as he went to his parents' bedroom, where his dad's desk was. There was a computer and printer on it. There was a giant calendar with his floor appointments. There were envelopes, some opened and some still sealed. There were pencils, pens, markers, catalogs, and a Bible. Z took a Post-it and wrote a note. "Please look at this. It's very important. I know it costs money, but I really want to enter this contest." He signed it with a big "Z," just like Zorro. Then he put it on the desk, hoping that it wouldn't be invisible, like him.

transposition—
a sleight allowing
the magician to secretly
trade one thing for
another

LOOP

WHEN LOOP GOT HOME, his mom said, "How did your audition go?"

"Fine."

"Did you have fun?"

"I guess."

She said, "Good. Now it's time to get to work. I want you to read the first chapter of a book I left by your door."

Loop saluted her and said, "Yes, ma'am," because his probation was more like a boot camp, even though in a *real* boot camp, soldiers did marching drills, push-ups, and obstacle courses. They fired guns and learned military strategy. They did not read books.

When he got to his room, he found a copy of *Frankenstein* propped against the door. At least his mom had respected the crime scene tape. Loop picked up the paperback and flipped through the pages. No pictures? Was she kidding? There were dozens of comic books about *Frankenstein*, but *his* mom got the version with no pictures.

He went to the kitchen, where she was chopping veggies for dinner. He waved the book in front of her face.

She said, "Oh, good. You found it. You've been drawing stitches on your body and painting your fingernails black."

"So?"

"So it reminded me of *Frankenstein*. That's why I want you to read that book."

"I already know the story, Mom. There's movies and everything."

"And movies are never as good as books."

He put *Frankenstein* on the counter. "But I only read *comic* books. I've told you a hundred times."

She put down the knife, placed her hands on her hips, and gave him the don't-talk-back-to-me look. "Is that right?"

"Absolutely." She looked at him a bit longer, and he looked at her. She didn't blink, and he didn't blink. She was a stone, not even breathing. She just kept staring at him, not blinking, and Loop tried to do the same, but it took all his concentration. Soon he was fidgeting. Couldn't help it. Over a minute had passed—a minute that felt longer than an hour. "Fine!" he said, giving in.

She picked up the knife again. "Since it doesn't have any pictures," she said over the sound of her chopping, "I want you to illustrate every chapter."

"Are you kidding?"

"*You're* the one who says you only read comic books. So turn this into a comic book."

He opened his mouth, but then shut it before getting into deeper trouble. The best choice was to head back to his room. He'd give anything to be at the magic shop, where he wouldn't have to think about books or his mom trying to teach him a lesson.

Loop removed the crime scene tape from his door and stepped in. He took off his shoes and dumped them in the corner. Then he plopped on his bed to read, but he fell asleep before the second page. He couldn't tell how long he had slept before he heard knocking.

Loop sat up, shook himself awake, and used his horror-film voice. "Enter at your own risk."

Rubén stepped in. "What's up?"

Loop said, "Not much. Just reading this stupid book as part of my penance."

"Hand it over. Let me see." Loop gave it to him, and Rubén studied the cover. "I read this a long time ago. It's a good book."

Loop shrugged. "If you say so."

Rubén stood there awhile, looking around the room like he'd never seen it before. Finally, he said, "So anything interesting happen today?"

Lots of interesting stuff happened, but no way was Loop telling Rubén. If that man could keep secrets about important stuff like *I'm not your real father*, then Loop could keep secrets about important stuff, too. So he said, "Just a normal day."

"How about watching the game later?"

If their favorite team, the San Antonio Spurs, won tonight, they'd be in the finals. Loop said, "Maybe," but he intentionally made the "maybe" sound like a "no." He lifted the book. "Gotta read. Mom's orders."

"Okay," Rubén said. He started to head out, but before leaving, he said, "Let me know if there's anything you need."

Loop remembered the magic contest. "Actually, I *do* need something."

Rubén seemed happy to hear this. Loop had to take advantage, so he showed him the form from Mr. Garza and explained all about the contest, how he'd be really, really happy, and how he was bound to learn the value of hard work if he was going to get good enough to perform in front of a bunch of people. And besides, his friends were entering, too, and they needed him for their team.

"We'll have to stay in Houston for a few days," Loop explained.

Rubén said, "I like going to Houston."

"So I can enter?"

"Of course. I'm going to check out the website and talk to Mr. Garza first, but I think it's a great idea."

Rubén was smiling, and Loop was smiling back. For a moment, he forgot the past few months. He almost hugged Rubén, but then he remembered. Rubén was not his dad, and no way was Loop hugging someone who wasn't blood. Besides, he was still mad. You weren't supposed to be nice to someone if you were mad, because then they'd think it was okay to hurt you. You had to be careful. You had to resist them. Or else they'd turn around and hurt you again.

Before it got too awkward, Loop picked up the book. "Better get back to reading," he said.

Rubén nodded. Then he left, gently closing the door behind him. Soon, Loop could hear Rubén and his mom talking, but with his door closed, he didn't know what they were saying.

He got back to the book. His eyes went over the words, but who knew what was happening. Something about a ship and the Arctic. Who cared? He was too busy imagining the contest and the moment when they announced that he and his friends had won. It *had* to be them. He'd already had a year of bad news, so *something* had to go right.

Something *had* to go right. But not today, because now his mom and Rubén were fighting, and their voices were loud enough for Loop to understand.

She said, "I can't believe you gave him permission for that contest without talking to me first."

And Rubén said, "What's the problem? It's going to be fun."

She said, "But you're spoiling him."

And he said, "No, I'm not."

And then she said, "You buy him everything he asks for. Ever since he found out, you've been trying to buy his love."

Loop hated how they talked behind his back. Even his cousins, aunts, and uncles did this. And they all laughed at him. *Of course they did*, he thought, *because I was a fool who couldn't see the truth when it was staring me in the face.* He hated this whole situation, the way his mom had done this sneaky transposition of fathers as easily as a magician trades cards in a trick. Loop didn't even know his real dad's name. His mom wouldn't tell him. She just said, "I was stupid. I made a mistake."

So, yeah, maybe Rubén was spoiling him, but Loop deserved to be spoiled after being humiliated in front of his whole family. Didn't people go to court to sue for emotional distress? Well, Loop was more distressed than the stray, flea-bitten dogs yapping at the pound. Who could blame him for wanting to make his mom and Rubén pay?

The Vernon Touch—
performing sleights
in a way that looks
natural

LOOP

THE FOLLOWING WEEK, LOOP and his friends returned to Conjuring Cats. They gave quick hellos to Mrs. Garza and Ariel and then headed straight to the Vault. Once again, Mr. Garza was wearing his baseball cap and tapping on his keyboard.

"Just a minute," he said. "I have to reply to these e-mails."

So the boys sat at a table to wait.

"My brother was sleepwalking again," Z said. "I woke up, and there he was, sitting at the foot of the bed."

"Was he staring at you?" Loop asked.

"No. His back was to me. He was staring at the closet door. Creeps me out just thinking about it. I turned on the lights, shook him, even got my other brother to clap in his face. When he finally woke up, he couldn't remember how he got there."

"So it's like he's possessed," Loop concluded. "Like in those paranormal movies."

"Don't say that. You're creeping me out again."

"Possessed. Possessed. Possessed!" Loop repeated, using his horror-film voice.

Z covered his ears. "Can't hear you!"

"Sleepwalking is a lot more common in kids than in adults," Dominic said. "I was reading about it."

Loop wanted to yawn. Every time an interesting subject came up, Dominic had to spoil it with facts.

"Why were you reading about sleepwalking?" Loop asked. "Was this for school?"

"No."

"You mean you were reading for *fun*? Because if you like reading for fun, I can give you my copy of *Frankenstein* and you can break it down chapter by chapter so I can draw some pictures."

"I just like reading sometimes," Dominic said. "It's not

exactly fun. More like...interesting. And I wasn't reading about sleepwalking. I was reading about murders and people who don't have to go to jail 'by reason of insanity' because it turns out that you don't know what you're doing when you're asleep, so you can't control yourself. Then I got curious about sleepwalking and Googled it."

Z's eyes widened. "So now you're saying my brother can kill me in my sleep and not even go to jail for it?"

"It's very rare," Dominic explained. "Most sleepwalkers don't actually walk anywhere. They just sit up in bed."

Loop had a *better* sleepwalking story. "My cousin," he said, "was sleepwalking one time. He had to pee, but instead of going to the bathroom, he went to his parents' room. They had this big square fan, but he thought it was the toilet. His pee flew everywhere and everyone got wet!"

"That's gross!" Z said, but he was laughing. The other two joined in, and their stomach muscles got sore from laughing so hard.

Just then, Mr. Garza cleared his throat. He stood right beside them. He definitely had stealth abilities.

"Do you want to be clowns or magicians?" he asked, straightening his T-shirt. Today his shirt had a picture of a German shepherd with the words ASSASSIN'S BREED written underneath. Loop nodded approvingly since this was obviously a reference to one of his favorite video games.

Mr. Garza was still waiting for their answer. "Well?"

The boys mumbled that they wanted to be magicians.

"Then read this."

He gave them a bunch of handouts stapled together. The top page said CHAPTER TWO: THE VERNON TOUCH.

Dominic grabbed a pencil and a highlighter from the backpack he carried around. He even brought out Post-its. *What a nerd!* Loop thought. *Why on earth would you bring school supplies to a magic shop?*

When Loop got the packet, he counted. "Thirteen pages!" he cried. "Thirteen pages and all single-spaced! You expect us to read this? I thought we were going to learn magic."

"No way!" Z said, quickly dropping the packet on the table, shaking his hands as if the pages had burned them. "Who gets homework when they're not even in school?"

Dominic had already highlighted a line. "Come on, guys. Maybe we'll learn something."

Mr. Garza didn't say anything. He just went back to his computer. So the boys started reading. At one point, Z said, "There's a lot of big words in here." At another point,

Loop said, "Cool! A one-handed magician!" A little later, Z came back with "Finally! Some pictures." And five minutes after that, Loop set down the packet and lowered his head to sleep, but Dominic shook him and Z clapped his hands. "Okay, okay," Loop said, lifting the packet again. They kept reading, with Z mumbling under his breath, Loop yawning, and Dominic taking notes.

Finally, all three announced that they had finished, so Mr. Garza left his computer and sat with them. "If you could pick three words or phrases to explain this chapter, what would they be?"

Loop answered first, counting off each word with his fingers. "Cure. For. Insomnia."

Sarcastic comments like this had gotten him in trouble at school, and Mr. Garza was not about to put up with Loop's nonsense, either. He lifted his glasses and stared at him. Then he said, "You want to try that again?"

So Loop did. This time he gave a *real* response. "Okay, so it's about one guy who does magic with his head, since he only has one hand. Then there's a guy who has *two* hands but he's all fidgety, so he does fidgety magic. And another guy does a French drop. At first, I thought a French drop was candy, like lemon drop or gumdrop, and probably because I'm really hungry right now. But it's not candy. It's a way of making a little ball or coin disappear. And the guy who does it has *two* hands. The handouts don't say that, but you can tell from the pictures."

Mr. Garza thought for a moment. "You're right about the French drop, and I can tell you read the chapter, at least the first half. But"—he paused—"I was hoping for three words or phrases that capture the main points."

That's when Z jumped in. "Slydini, Malini, and Cardini!"

Loop cracked up and gave his friend a fist bump.

Mr. Garza turned to him. "Those are names, young man. I'm looking for something you learned about magic."

"But I *did* learn something," Z argued. "If you want to be a magician, your name has to end with *-ini*. So maybe my magic name can be Zalini."

"Or Zucchini," Loop suggested. He and Z laughed even harder.

Mr. Garza knocked on the table to get their attention. "Let's focus on the *real* lessons in this chapter. He nodded toward Dominic. "What phrases would *you* pick?"

Dominic flipped through the packet. Loop couldn't believe what he saw. Not only had Dominic used a high-lighter, but he also had written notes in the margins!

"I'd pick 'use your head,' 'be natural,' and 'practice, practice, practice,'" Dominic said.

"Excellent!" Mr. Garza replied.

Loop was tempted to write "know-it-all" on a Post-it and stick it on Dominic's forehead, but then he remembered his probation. The last thing he needed was to get kicked out of Conjuring Cats for silly antics, so he kept his comments to himself.

mentor—
someone with experience
who teaches and offers
advice to people
interested in learning
the craft

DOMINIC

DOMINIC WAS EMBARRASSED AGAIN. Why did his friends turn everything into a joke? Couldn't they be serious for once? Mr. Garza was sharing some very important information, but Loop and Z were only half listening. *I guess it's up to me to pay attention and explain things later,* Dominic thought with a sigh.

Mr. Garza went on to discuss how magic isn't just gimmicks and tricks but a real art that requires a lot of thinking. First, you have to figure out which sleights to use and then how to perform them, keeping in mind that everyone has limitations.

The magician with one hand was a good example. He couldn't do sleights like everyone else. He had to change them to fit his body. That's why the chapter mentioned a fidgety magician, too. Being fidgety was normal for him, so he worked it into his routine. Mr. Garza said that when you learned a sleight, you made it fit *you*, not the other way around. This was what the famous magician Dai Vernon, also known as the Professor, meant when he said, "Be natural."

After explaining this, Mr. Garza got quiet for a few moments. Then he asked each of the boys a lot of questions: What do you think about when you daydream? What interests you? Are you shy or daring or a snob? But also, what size are your hands? Are they relaxed or stiff? When you stand, do you move around a lot or mostly stay still?

Loop and Z managed to answer the questions without being silly, so Dominic relaxed a bit.

Then Mr. Garza went to a shelf and grabbed a handful of DVDs. He didn't play them or even open them. He showed Dominic and his friends the covers and talked about the magicians who were featured—how Max Maven has a deep, hypnotic voice that goes well with his mind-reading tricks and how Jay Sankey is a prankster who loves to perform tricks that make people laugh. And even though Mr. Garza was acting like a schoolteacher and the Vault had suddenly become a classroom, Dominic didn't mind, because this kind of learning was fun.

"So now for your homework," Mr. Garza said, and no one complained. "First, think about your interests. Second, observe yourself to see how you move. Third, learn the French drop."

"Like on the handout?" Loop asked.

"Exactly."

Everyone flipped to the page that demonstrated the French drop. They studied the pictures while Mr. Garza grabbed four small balls from a bin. Before returning to the table, he took off his baseball cap and grabbed a large red sombrero that hung on the wall. It was very fancy, with gold trim on the edges and golden starbursts stitched into the brim.

"When I wear this hat," he said, "I am no longer Mr. Garza. I am Señor Surprise, magician and former president of the Texas Association of Magicians, and a member of the Royal Order of Willard, which grants me the privilege of free breakfast during the convention. I am, in short, an award-winning performer in the United States...and *beyond*." Here he paused, and even though he was looking at the ceiling, Dominic could tell he was *really* looking at the entire sky.

He gave each of the boys a little red ball and kept one

for himself. "Observe carefully," he said. He held the ball between his thumb and forefinger and made a big deal of showing it to the boys. He brought the ball to his nose and sniffed it, his mustache twitching like rabbit whiskers. He put it in his mouth. Dominic could see the bulge on Señor Surprise's cheek as he moved the ball around. Then he swallowed it, choking a bit because it was so large. When he finally got it down, he opened his mouth and stuck out his tongue to prove that the ball had disappeared. Then his mustache started to twitch again, this time in a way that pointed at Señor Surprise's left ear. That's when Dominic understood his name, because Señor Surprise got a very surprised expression on his face. He started shaking his head like people do when water gets in their ears. Then he tugged at his earlobe, and guess what rolled out—the little red ball! The boys couldn't help but clap. They were impressed.

"Now for the French drop," Señor Surprise said.

"You mean that wasn't the French drop?" Z asked.

"No, that was me being silly." The boys laughed. With his Meathead baseball cap, Mr. Garza was all business, but with his sombrero, he was all fun.

He showed them the French drop. His technique looked exactly like the pictures in the handout. He held the ball in one hand and grabbed it with the other. Then the ball disappeared. Of course, it didn't *really* disappear. The sleight was supposed to let you hide the ball in your hands so that you could *pretend* it was gone.

It looked easy, but when the boys tried, they all messed up. Z dropped the ball every time, and he had to chase it as it rolled across the floor. Loop's hands were too stiff, so even though he could do the move, he had trouble hiding the ball. Dominic was the only one who could perform the sleight, but it took him a whole minute instead of a few seconds because he thought about every single part of the move.

Mr. Garza nodded thoughtfully. Then he took off his sombrero and put his baseball cap back on. "Let me show you how," he said. He worked with them, one by one, demonstrating the sleight and positioning their hands. Dominic understood what to do, but it was tough. When Mr. Garza did the French drop, it looked like magic. When *Dominic* did it, you could tell he was trying to hide something because he moved so slowly.

"You're not being natural," Mr. Garza said to the boys. "Remember, you have to be natural." He gave them more pointers, and then he said, "Now it's just a matter of practice. You must keep doing this until it's perfect and you can do it without thinking."

"But that's impossible," Z cried. "I *have* to think. I'm thinking *really* hard right now."

"It *is* possible," Dominic said. "Remember when we were learning how to ride our bikes? How hard it was, but how easy it is now?"

"That's right," Loop said. "I never think when I ride my bike. I just do it."

"I guess," Z agreed. "Like when I couldn't tie my shoelaces."

"Or write your name," Dominic added.

"Or escape from the Temple of No Return on the *Monument Maze* video game," Z said.

Dominic's shoulders dropped. No matter how hard he tried, he couldn't escape the Temple of No Return, and it really bugged him that he hadn't solved the puzzles. It didn't seem possible for Z to figure them out first, not when Dominic was the smart one. That's why he felt certain that Z had help from one of his older brothers, which was the same thing as cheating as far as Dominic was concerned.

"It's supereasy to escape, so maybe it'll be supereasy to do the French drop after a while," Z said.

Dominic and Loop just rolled their eyes. It was rude for Z to rub his *Monument Maze* success in their faces.

Mr. Garza had more work to do, so he returned to his

computer, but the boys kept practicing, trying to help one another. Dominic told his friends that it was easier if they started with their palms facing up. Loop told them that closing the gaps between their fingers helped hide the ball, and Z mentioned that it's more natural to look at the empty hand, and not at the hand that's secretly hiding the ball.

Once in a while, one of them did an excellent French drop, and the others cheered. But it was hard to get it right every single time. "We can't give up," they told one another. "We have to keep trying." Dominic mentally listed all the people who didn't give up when things got tough: Batman, Iron Man, Wolverine, Navy SEALs, UFC fighters, ninjas, Harry Potter, and Abraham Lincoln.

Meanwhile, Ariel had stepped into the Vault. She had stealth abilities just like her father, so Dominic didn't see her at first. But eventually he noticed her. She stood at the curtained doorway with her notebook. And as she watched and listened to everything Dominic and his friends said, she scribbled down notes.

She did not look happy.

palm—
to secretly conceal
something in your
hand

FOR TWO WHOLE WEEKS, Z practiced the French drop, plus a few other sleights. His friends were getting better at the tricks, too. Loop had bought a chop cup that made balls appear and disappear. He'd also bought a quarter shell, which he gave to Dominic, but because Dominic preferred mentalism, he'd stuck it in his locker and forgotten about it.

In Z's opinion, all you needed for impressive magic was a deck of cards. That's what he spent all his time on. He'd almost mastered palming and pinkie breaks already. In fact, every time he had a free moment, he practiced card sleights and studied routines on YouTube or in books from Mr. Garza's library. There were so many tricks you could perform with a simple deck. And cards weren't expensive at all—except for trick decks or gaff cards (which you could make yourself, if you wanted). Luckily, Loop was nice enough to buy Z a Svengali deck, and Z couldn't wait to learn how to use it.

They met at Dominic's apartment nearly every day and walked to Conjuring Cats from there. They hadn't figured out their routine for the competition yet, so they gave themselves a schedule. While Dominic was in Corpus (he was leaving the next day), they'd brainstorm, and when he returned in two weeks, they'd find a way to merge all their ideas.

Z knew that by teaming up with his friends, he had a better chance of getting first place. "I hope we get more than a ribbon," he said. "All I ever get is ribbons when I compete in things."

"That's because you never win," Loop said. "You just *participate*."

"I win sometimes!" Z wanted to offer an example, but he couldn't think of one.

Loop said, "I bet we get a big trophy."

"That'd be cool," Z said. "What does a magic trophy look like anyway?"

"Probably a giant cup," Dominic suggested. "Have you ever noticed that trophies are shaped like cups even for stuff that has nothing to do with drinking?"

Z had to admit that Dominic was right again—trophies *did* look like giant cups.

"At least there's such a thing as cups and balls in magic," Dominic went on, "so a giant cup makes a *little* bit of sense."

"Maybe the trophy is shaped like a top hat or a wizard's hat," Z said.

"Or a thumb tip," Loop added, and they all laughed at the idea of a trophy in the shape of a giant thumb.

"We better not get a certificate," Z said. "They're the lamest awards you can get."

Loop laughed. "I made a paper airplane out of the last certificate I got." He pretended to throw a plane and made exploding sounds to show that it had crashed.

"What'd you get a certificate for?" Dominic asked. It was a good question, because Loop was always in trouble at school.

"Most Likely to Start a Garage Band," Loop answered.

"But you don't even play an instrument," Z said.

"Exactly!" Loop lifted his chin and showed them the fake stitches he'd drawn on his neck. Then he showed them his hands. Every other fingernail was black. "I think they were talking about my style. I guess people who start garage bands look like me."

"Well," Z said, "I'd rather get a certificate for Most Likely to Start a Garage Band than Most Likely to Be a Pop Star."

"But that sounds like a compliment," Dominic said.

"Not when you don't get it for singing."

"Why'd you get it, then?"

"Because I drink soda pop during lunch. Get it? I'm a *pop* star."

His friends laughed. Z laughed, too, even though the joke was on him. Then he wondered why teachers were so desperate to give awards, even to the slackers. Loop said the teachers were taking bribes from parents, and Dominic said they were just trying to help kids with their self-esteem.

"In a real competition," Loop explained, "you don't get anything for just participating. Like in the Olympics. There's gold, silver, and bronze. Sometimes they don't even bother with bronze. My dad—I mean, Rubén—took us to a chili cook-off, and there was a winner and a runner-up. That's it."

They arrived at Conjuring Cats. They stepped inside and said hello to Mrs. Garza before going to the Vault, where Ariel was practicing with a dancing cane in front of a full-size mirror. Z remembered a video of David Copperfield doing this routine. That guy could make a cane dance in midair, but Ariel wasn't having any luck because the cane kept hitting the floor. She didn't drop it exactly, but it sure didn't look like Copperfield's routine. She started over. For a few seconds, the cane floated between her hands, but when she tried to make it dance, it hit the floor again.

Her moves looked clumsy, so Z giggled. But Dominic tried to encourage her. "You almost had it that time."

She had her back to them, but she could see their reflections in the mirror. "Almost isn't good enough," she said. Then she put her cane away and headed to the curtained door. Ariel usually left the Vault as soon as the boys arrived.

Z said, "You can stay if you want. Maybe you can show us some tricks."

She turned and glared at him. "Magicians *never* share their secrets."

"Sure, they do," Mr. Garza said. He was at his computer

on YouTube. "But only with people who are serious about the craft. Like these boys. They're getting better every day."

Ariel crossed her arms. "Are they now?"

"Yeah! Look at this," Z said.

He wanted to redeem himself after dropping cards the first time he tried a cascade, so he took out his deck and palmed a card. He did a great job of hiding it in his hand, but instead of clapping, Ariel rolled her eyes and said, "Big deal. You haven't even put that in a routine."

Before Z had time to respond, Mr. Garza said, "Here it is!" He waved them over. Everyone except Ariel gathered around the computer, though instead of exiting the Vault, she went to the counter on the far side of the room, jumped up, and sat there with her legs dangling.

Meanwhile, Mr. Garza started the video. "This magician is named Bill Malone. Pay careful attention." Z and his friends leaned forward. When the video started, there wasn't any sound. Z wondered why Mr. Garza had forgotten to turn up the volume, but he didn't want to embarrass him, so he didn't mention it.

On the video, Malone sat at a table and shuffled cards. He then threw out four kings. After cutting the deck, he revealed four queens. He kept shuffling, talking, and cutting the deck. Z wished he knew what the guy was saying because the audience was laughing. Malone repeatedly mixed up the cards and threw out a few. They seemed totally random—six, five, four, two, and then a three and a nine. Sometimes Malone did one-handed cuts, and little by little, the deck in his hands got smaller while the pile on the table got larger. Finally, when all the cards were in a messy pile, the audience clapped and Malone thumped his chest like a gorilla.

"Did you like that?" Mr. Garza asked. He winked at Ariel, but she just turned away.

Z glanced at his friends. They seemed just as confused as he was, but after a few moments, Dominic answered the question. "I like how the magician did a lot of shuffles and flourishes before throwing out the cards."

"That one-handed cut is textbook," Loop added, "and he has a great ribbon spread, too."

Z wrinkled his forehead. How did Loop know about one-handed cuts and ribbon spreads? Those were card terms, but Loop didn't like cards. That was Z's domain. Z was supposed to talk about the guy's card handling, but once again, his friends had pushed him aside, leaving him with nothing to say.

Mr. Garza looked at him. "What did *you* think?"

At that point, Z was confused, since his friends had already given answers—answers that should have come from *him*—so he said, "I don't know. It's hard to follow when you can't hear what the guy's saying. I mean, what's the point of throwing out random cards?"

"Aha!" Mr. Garza's finger pointed at the sky. "But are they *truly* random?"

This sounded like a deep philosophical question, so Z thought about it—seriously—but in the end, he could only shrug. He didn't know anything about deep philosophical questions.

"Let's watch again," Mr. Garza suggested.

This time, he turned on the volume. Malone was talking about a guy named Sam the Bellhop, and he began his tale, the whole time shuffling, cutting, and throwing out cards. When Malone said, "Four gentlemen walked into the hotel dressed as kings," he threw out four kings. When he said, "They were joined by two brunettes and two redheads," he threw out the black queens and then the red ones. Every time Malone mentioned a number, he threw out the matching cards. Z was amazed by Malone's ability to predict the next card. He said, "Sam went to the 654 Club," as he threw out a six, a five, and a four. He said, "Sam got a two-dollar tip," as he threw out a two. He said, "Sam was thirty-nine," as he threw out a three and a nine. Finally, all the cards in the deck had been mentioned in the story, and that's when Malone thumped his chest.

Z and his friends laughed, not only because they had enjoyed the trick but also because Malone's chest thumping looked silly.

Once again, Mr. Garza wanted to know if they liked the performance.

The boys nodded, and Z rushed to speak before his friends stole his ideas again. "I'm not confused anymore," he said, all proud.

"Well, duh," Ariel called from her spot on the counter. "Of course you're not confused, since you can hear him now. That's the most obvious thing you could say."

Z's shoulders slumped. Why couldn't he do anything right?

patter—
what a magician says
while performing
a trick

DOMINIC

DOMINIC WANTED TO SHARE his insights about the Malone routine, how his trick seemed to use a combination of mentalism *and* sleights, and how well Malone interacted with the audience, something Dominic was still trying to figure out. But now Ariel was challenging her father again, and all because of Z's dumb comment.

"Is this what you do all day?" she asked her dad. "Show them videos—sound off, sound on?"

Luckily, Mr. Garza ignored her and went on with his lesson. "Let's talk about patter," he said. Dominic wrote "patter" in a spiral notebook he carried around. He wanted to remember *everything* he learned in the Vault.

Patter, Mr. Garza explained, was what a magician *said* while performing a trick. Sometimes, he told a story. Sometimes, he told jokes. Sometimes, he just told you what he was going to do. But, no matter what kind of patter the magician used, he had a certain attitude. Maybe he acted like a wise man or a clown. Maybe he poked fun at himself or maybe he poked fun at the audience. Most important, however, was that what the magician *said* had to match what he *did*.

"You can have a hundred versions of the same routine," Mr. Garza said, "if you change the patter." He looked at Ariel. "My daughter, for example, is very good at taking common tricks and making them her own."

"I do *not* rip people off," Ariel insisted. "I come up with my own stuff."

"That's exactly what I said," her father answered. Dominic had to agree. Why couldn't Ariel see the compliment?

"No, you didn't," she said. "You accused me of *common* tricks, but I'm not using cheap, plastic props from beginner magic kits." She glanced at Dominic and his friends—that's what they did to get the keys for the Vault. "Anybody can learn the Hot Rod or Pen-through-Dollar tricks. What *I* do is unique—and a lot more advanced."

"You're missing my point," Mr. Garza said.

"Oh yeah? Well, you're missing *mine*!"

Now it was *his* turn to roll his eyes. Ariel just huffed, all annoyed.

Mr. Garza turned back to the boys. "Good patter," he continued, "can take a simple trick and turn it into art. *¿Entiendes?*"

Dominic nodded as he wrote "trick w/ good patter = art."

"So this week," Mr. Garza said, "I want you to study how the magicians handle props *and* what they say while they're doing their tricks. Then I want you to go back to the French drop and add patter. Any questions?" The boys didn't ask anything, so Mr. Garza shooed them away from his desk. "Go, go. Practice. And feel free to read any of the books or view any of the DVDs. I recommend Eugene Burger. He makes excellent use of patter."

The boys went to his shelves to browse through the collection, while Mr. Garza got back to work.

Since there were so many books and DVDs, Dominic didn't know where to start. "What do you recommend?" he asked Ariel. Nearly every day, he asked for her opinion. She never offered it, but that didn't stop him from trying.

This time, however, she *did* answer. She stopped swinging her legs and began to speak. "Well, personally, I don't think patter is necessary. I managed to win the competition without saying a single word. There's patter and there's performance, and in my mind, they are two separate things."

"She makes a good point," her father said. He still faced his computer, and once again, Dominic realized that he could work while listening to everything they said.

Ariel actually smiled a little. She was a lot prettier with a smile than with a smirk.

"I'm most inspired by the Japanese magicians," she went on. "Yumi Nakajima and Hiroki Hara. They travel all over the world to perform. Imagine visiting so many countries. You can't possibly learn the languages, and having an interpreter is just awkward. So you have to do a routine without patter. That way, no matter where you are, the audience will follow. If your trick relies on patter and your audience doesn't know the language, then they're going to be confused, like you guys when you were watching that video with Bill Malone." Dominic nodded, and he and his friends waited as she thought more about this topic. "Having a routine without patter is like telling a story without words," she concluded. "It's . . . it's . . . *pure*."

The boys were silent for a while. Then Loop said, "That's deep." He sounded all impressed.

Mr. Garza had swiveled around while she spoke. Now he was smiling, and when Ariel noticed, she smiled back. Dominic had no idea why they fought all the time, since they both loved magic. For a moment, he thought that Ariel and her father had finally settled their differences—that they'd stop bickering and work as a team. He even dared to hope that she'd hang out in the Vault and help them, too, because—well—she was pretty.

But then Mr. Garza said, "Why don't you show them videos of magicians you admire? Then you can explain why."

And at this, Ariel's pleasant smile morphed into a cranky scowl. "Why don't *you* show them?" she said. "*I've* got work to do."

Mr. Garza could only sigh. He seemed supremely disappointed, but he didn't scold her. Instead, he just swiveled back to his computer.

Dominic thought Ariel would leave for sure now, but she didn't. Still, she made a big show of pretending they were not there as she grabbed her cane and faced the mirror to practice again.

So he and his friends returned to the shelves and took a bunch of videos to the table. As they scanned the covers, they talked a little more about the contest awards.

"I bet we don't get a ribbon, a trophy, *or* a certificate," Dominic said. "I bet we get money."

Loop cheered. "That's even better! I can finally get surround sound in my room. It will totally optimize our video game experience."

"And I can get us tickets to Schlitterbahn so we can try out the Boogie Bahn," Dominic said.

Z looked at his faded Tony Hawk T-shirt. "I just want new clothes. I'm tired of wearing hand-me-downs."

Dominic didn't know what to say about that. Sometimes, he felt sorry for Z, but then again, Z's parents weren't divorced. He had an entire family to hang out with, and they were a lot more fun than Dominic's mom.

"So how much do you think we'll win?" Loop asked. "A million bucks?"

"No," Dominic answered. "They probably won't give a million bucks to a bunch of kids. We'll probably get a thousand dollars or something like that."

"We can do a lot with a thousand dollars," Z said.

In addition to new clothes, he suggested tablets and Google Play cards. He also suggested getting a German shepherd, one of the ones that had worked for the police because they were trained and wouldn't pee on their shoes.

At the mention of police, Loop said they should get a police scanner so they could hear about the crimes around town, especially ones with lots of blood and guts, and Dominic suggested they set up a fund to help the victims. They were on a roll, listing ways to spend the prize money. Meanwhile, Ariel gave up on her cane and approached the table, and when Loop mentioned hiring a private jet to fly them to Disney World, she said, "Oh, please! That's ridiculous."

"So what would *you* do with the money?" Dominic asked.

"It's irrelevant, since you don't get any money. You get a trophy if you really have to know, and it's in the shape of a giant cup."

Dominic *knew* it! Oh well, at least it was better than a ribbon or a certificate.

Loop said, "One of you can keep the trophy. I don't think a big cup is going to look good in my room."

"I don't have a place to store it," Z said. "Not with all my brothers' junk around."

Dominic sighed. "I guess I can take it to Corpus," he said. "My little sister is always asking for stuff. Besides, it's not about the trophy. It's about winning."

At that, the boys gave one another fist bumps.

"OMG!" Ariel exclaimed. "You guys are clueless."

"What do you mean?" Z wanted to know.

"You guys are not a team of magicians like Penn and Teller. You're competing *against* one another, and guess what!" She smiled—not a proud or happy smile but a mean one. "Only *one* of you gets to win."

Dominic and his friends were speechless. They loved to compete, especially against one another, but video games, races, and silly challenges didn't matter. Those were just games, while this contest was for real. They wanted to be a team. How could they possibly compete *against* one another? And how could Dominic compete all alone? He had stage fright. He'd throw up on the judges for sure!

cut—

to tear something apart; in magic, a cut refers to dividing a deck of cards

LOOP

AFTER LOOP AND HIS friends left Conjuring Cats, they went a whole block without saying a word. Finally, Z broke the silence.

"Maybe there's a way we can compete as a team. Some musicians have bands, and others go solo. If it works for music, why can't it work for magic?"

"That's true," Loop said. "But think about the singing competitions like *American Idol*. It's *one* person competing, not a whole band."

Z wouldn't give up on his idea. "Okay, but in sports,

people compete against each other—in teams *and* by themselves."

Loop was not convinced. "But sports have rules that control whether they have teams. Can you imagine playing one-on-one football, or a bunch of dudes cramped in the same car for the Indy 500?"

Then Z said, "Maybe I can't imagine one-on-one football, but I *can* imagine one-on-one basketball. *Plenty* of sports have both solo and team events."

Loop couldn't believe it. This guy would not give up. "Like what?" he asked, because he couldn't think of any examples.

"Like tennis, track, swimming, and gymnastics," Z answered.

Loop threw up his arms. "That still doesn't make any sense!" he said. "Sure, you have relays in track, but you never have a single guy running against a whole relay team."

Then Dominic offered his opinion. "I think competing as a team is a great idea, but we'd have to look at the rules to see if it's allowed."

Loop shook his head. "Face it, guys. This magic competition is not a team sport. Just like Ariel said."

"But it *might* be," Z said, all hopeful. "We just have to

look at the rules, like Dominic suggested. Maybe there's a team category."

"Well, if there is," Loop said, "I'd have to be the leader." His friends glanced at him, all confused. Were they really that dense? "I'm the only one with money, remember? Plus, I already turned in my registration form. 'First come, first served' is what I say."

"No," Dominic said. "If we work as a team, *I* should be the leader, since you two are slackers when it comes to using your neurons."

"I use my neurons!" Z said, but then he added, "Wait, what's a neuron?"

Dominic tapped his head.

"I use my head!"

Dominic laughed. "How can you say that, when every time you get a set of instructions, you need *me* to figure them out?"

"We don't *need* you to figure them out," Loop said. "You're the one who's always grabbing the instructions and acting like you know it all."

"Besides, it takes a lot more than reading instructions to do magic," Z added. "You also need a personality. Without *my* advice, your tricks are boring."

"Well, without *my* advice," Dominic countered, "you wouldn't know step one of your routine."

"And without *me*," Loop said, "neither one of you would have any props to work with. You'd be doing *air* magic."

Dominic narrowed his eyes. "Fine. Don't come crying next time you need me to explain instructions that any third grader could follow. You're on your own from now on."

"Whatever," Z said. "I don't care. I've got enough people telling me what to do. The last thing I need is someone else acting like he's my brother or my dad."

They reached a big intersection with lots of traffic, so Dominic pressed the crosswalk button. "In that case, we can just forget about competing in the magic contest as a team. Even if there *is* a loophole."

"Sounds good to me," Loop said. "I thought it was a stupid idea all along."

"The *idea* wasn't stupid," Z said, all offended. "*You* guys are the ones who are stupid!"

"You're the one who's always asking dumb questions and giving dumb answers," Dominic said.

"Only because you guys never let me answer or perform or do anything *first*. By the time I have a chance to talk, all the good stuff has already been said."

The little walking man showed up on the street sign, and

Z ran across. He didn't even say good-bye, and when he got across the street, he kept running.

Loop chuckled.

"What's so funny?" Dominic asked.

"Don't you get it?" Loop said, but when he realized that Dominic had no idea why he was giggling, he went on. "This is a big fight over nothing. Let's face it. I'm the only one who's going to win, because I'm the only one who's actually going to the convention."

"Here we go again," Dominic said.

"What does *that* mean?"

"Sometimes, you're nothing but a show-off."

"No, I'm not."

"Then why are you always waving money in our faces?" Dominic said. "You know Z's family is broke."

"It's not my fault you guys are *pobres*."

"I'm not poor. My dad helps out. And guess what, he's my *real* dad. He doesn't have to prove anything."

Loop postured up for a fight. "Take that back!"

"Make me," Dominic said as the streetlight began to tick off the time—only five seconds left to cross the street. "Guess you'll have to catch the next light," he called as he raced off.

Sure enough, traffic started to move again, but Loop

didn't care. He was fighting mad. Show-off, huh? Maybe Loop *did* wave money in their faces, but that didn't stop his friends from taking it. They didn't even thank him when he gave them stuff. If he was a show-off, then they were leeches, and the only way to get rid of leeches was to pluck those bloodsuckers off.

writer's block—
when an author can't
think of what to write next;
it can also refer to when
an artist or performer
gets stuck while trying to
create something new

DOMINIC

WHEN HE WOKE UP the next morning, Dominic was so glad to be leaving town. He really needed a break from his friends. His mother was working a half day, and as soon as she got home, Dominic was going to be swapped. That's what he called it when his parents traded him off.

He grabbed his duffel bag. He already had clothes at his dad's house, so he used his bag for his PlayStation, video games, books, and some lecture notes that he had borrowed from Mr. Garza. It took about thirty minutes to get ready, so he had some time to kill before his mom came home.

He decided to work on patter for his French drop

routine. He took out his notebook and read through yesterday's brainstorm session, but all his ideas seemed lame. He couldn't get Z's voice out of his head, especially the comment about Dominic being boring. *He's just jealous because I'm smarter than he is*, Dominic thought. So what if he liked to read about canyons and planets and microorganisms? He didn't need Z for inspiration. He had science.

Wait a minute! That was the answer. He'd use science!

Dominic made a list of things he'd learned in school, and sure enough, he got a perfect idea for the French drop routine. He wrote out a little script, and then he started to practice. His French drop was almost perfect now. He even added gestures like pointing or wriggling his fingers, all while performing the sleight and making it look natural. Dominic had also taught himself the Hebrew rise, a move that let the ball reappear. But when he added patter, he struggled, because it was like he needed two brains—one to control his hands and one to control his mouth.

He stood in front of a mirror and held up a cotton ball. "This," he said to his imaginary audience, "is a rain cloud, and as it rains"—he did the French drop—"the cloud disappears." He opened his hand, finger by finger, to reveal an empty palm. "Then you have clear skies," he said, looking up and pointing with both hands, even with the one that secretly held the cotton ball. "But the rain puddles evaporate, and"—here he did the Hebrew rise by raising one hand, making sure it crossed the other so he could steal the hidden cotton ball—"the rain cloud reappears." He held his hand and the cotton ball high over his head.

His shoulders drooped. "The evaporation cycle?" he said to his reflection. "Really? That is so lame!"

He decided to ditch the idea. It was back to the drawing board, but he was *still* staring at a blank page when his mom came home. Luckily, she was eager to hit the road. Dominic couldn't be more relieved. He had a severe case of writer's block, but maybe a change of scenery would help.

His mom didn't say much as she drove, and if the scenery could talk, it'd be quiet, too—nothing but flat land, cows, and an occasional train to look at.

"I can't wait to show Dad my magic tricks," Dominic said. When he saw his mother rub her temple, he asked if she was getting a headache.

"No," she answered. "Just tired. Long week at work."

She was always tired after work. It made no sense. After all, she worked as a receptionist, which meant sitting at a desk all day and answering phones. His dad, on the other hand, was an engineer for the city. He sat at a computer *and* visited sites, but he still had energy to go fishing, host barbecues, and watch sports on TV when he got home. He even played hopscotch and dress-up with Maria Elena. When Dominic mentioned this to his mom, she said that her workday didn't end at five o'clock because she had to work at the apartment, too. But as far as Dominic was concerned, *he* was the one who did chores at the apartment. All his mom did was cook and clean up the kitchen.

They finally reached the Burger King in Refugio where Dominic's dad waited on a bench with the latest issue of *Field & Stream*. His mom parked nearby. Then his parents smiled and waved, but that's it. His dad stayed on the bench, and his mom stayed in the car.

"Have fun," she said. Then, "If you get homesick and want to come home early, let me know. I'll come get you."

"I never get homesick when I go to Corpus," Dominic said.

"I know, but just in case."

Dominic opened the car door, but before he stepped out, he said, "Why don't you come talk to Dad for a while? We can get some fries at Burger King."

She shook her head. "Maybe next time. I should hurry back now."

"That's what you *always* say, but 'next time' never comes. Just come and chat for five minutes. I'll be there, too."

"I'm sure your dad wants to get back to his family," she said.

Dominic sighed. Would his parents *ever* talk? What was so hard about saying hello and discussing the weather? Even *strangers* talked about the weather. It was a universal topic because you could always say, "Wonder if it's going to rain" or "It's mighty hot, ain't it?"

"Be good," his mom said, pressing the button to open the trunk. "And send me a text when you get there so I know you arrived safely, okay?"

"I promise," Dominic said, leaning over to kiss her cheek.

Then he got out of the car, grabbed his duffel bag, and waved good-bye as his mom drove away.

His dad wasn't the hugging type. Instead, he said, "Hey, buddy," and reached out for a handshake, only it wasn't a real handshake. He and Dominic bumped fists straight on, then top and bottom, and finally a high five, a low five, and a playful punch to the gut.

"Let's get this show on the road," his dad said.

They got in the car, and as they headed out, Dominic's dad rambled about the NBA finals and the weather. "I just know we're going to get the big one this year," he said about hurricanes.

"What if it knocks down the whole city?" Dominic asked, and they went on about doomsday scenarios and survival plans as they drove along a small country road where Dominic sometimes spotted javelinas, coyotes, or bobcats (once he saw a bobcat with a rabbit in its mouth), then through Bayside, a small town with a boat ramp and bait house since it was a favorite fishing spot, then through miles of cotton and wheat fields, and finally past hundreds of giant white windmills. At last they reached the major highway, and the last leg of the trip took them over the Harbor Bridge and into Corpus Christi.

"So what have you been up to this summer?" his dad asked as they drove into the city. "You still doing magic?" The last time Dominic had visited, he'd shown them his Hot Rod routine.

"Of course."

"I knew it! I've been telling my friends about you."

"Tell them the next Houdini is in the house," Dominic said.

"You know it!" his dad cheered.

Dominic saw an opportunity. "So that's what I want to talk to you about," he began.

"You want me to handcuff you and lock you in a crate so you can try to get out?"

Dominic laughed.

"Sounds like fun," his dad teased.

"It does, but seriously, I want to ask you something."

"Shoot."

Dominic reached into his pocket and pulled out the registration form for the contest, even though he knew his dad couldn't read it while driving. "Okay, so there's this magic convention at the end of the summer. They're going to have lectures and shows and a competition for teens like me. So can I go?"

His dad didn't skip a beat. "You bet you can go!"

"Are you sure?"

"You bet I'm sure!"

"Because it costs money."

"*No problemo*," his dad said with a Texan accent instead of a Spanish one. "What *doesn't* cost money?"

By the time they reached the house, Dominic's dad was full of plans. "We'll *all* go to Houston, so you can have your own cheering section," and, "We have to brainstorm stage names. How about Dominic the Dominant?"

"The dominant what?" Dominic laughed.

"Oh, I don't know. I'm sure we can figure something out."

As soon as they stepped into the house, Dominic's sister ran to the door. "He's here! He's here! He's here!" She threw her arms around him.

"Nice to see you, too," Dominic said.

He wanted to swing her around, but she was getting too big for that, so he tickled her instead. Then his stepmom came in.

"Hello," she said, kissing his forehead.

The whole family got into the car so they could go to the two-story Whataburger on Shoreline Drive. Dominic loved sitting outside on the second floor because you could see the ocean. After dinner, they took a walk along the seawall and pointed out the sights—cargo ships, fishermen, skateboarders and in-line skaters, seagulls, and so many families enjoying the sea breeze. Maria Elena got tired after a while, so Dominic gave her a piggyback ride. He was having so much fun with his Corpus Christi family that he forgot to text his mom, and because he was laughing so hard at his dad's jokes, he didn't hear his phone beep when his mom sent a note to ask if he had reached the house yet.

magician in trouble—
a magician who
pretends to make
mistakes during his or her
performance

Z HAD FINALLY MASTERED the French drop. In fact, he could do it without thinking. It was like riding a bicycle or reading. Once you knew how, you wondered why it was so hard at the beginning. But Mr. Garza wanted more. He wanted Z to come up with a routine and patter, and doing that was harder than all of last year's homework assignments combined. How could Z come up with patter when he didn't know any French? He got a headache just thinking about it. Why couldn't the move be called the Spanish drop? He knew plenty of Spanish. Or better yet, the

English drop? Isn't that what he spoke all the time? But no. It was called the French drop, so that was the language he wanted to use—never mind that the only French phrase he knew was *excusez-moi* and only because of the snobby girls at school. "*Excusez-moi*," they'd say as they pushed their way through the crowded hall or interrupted the teacher in the middle of a sentence. So he figured it meant "excuse me" but also "I'm sorry," since they said it when pretending to apologize for passing notes or making fun of someone.

Like the way his friends made fun of his idea a few days ago. They definitely owed him an *excusez-moi*. But what was he thinking? They didn't know French, either, not even Dominic the Brainiac. Z laughed to himself when he imagined Dominic pulling out his hair as he tried to come up with something as clever as French patter. Knowing a bunch of facts was useless if you didn't have an imagination, Z decided.

He was determined to prove how creative he could be, so he got to work on his routine. First, he needed a French guy. Z took a small rubber ball and drew a face on it. In all the cartoons, French guys had thin mustaches and wore berets, so Z added a downward "V" for the mustache. Then he raided his sisters' room to see if their Barbies had berets, but they didn't have dolls anymore—only makeup and jewelry. "I guess you don't get a hat," he said to the ball, making it nod back. He stared at it for a while. "Hello, Pierre," he said, since it was the only French-sounding name he could think of.

That's when Boxer Boy stepped into the room. "Who are you talking to?" he asked. He was in his *chones*, their word for underwear, because he'd just showered, so he went straight to the dresser for some clothes.

Z closed his hand around the ball. "No one."

"C'mon. Let me see what you have. Is it a cricket?"

"No."

"A roach?" His brother started hopping around and singing. "*La cucaracha, la cucaracha, ya no puede caminar.*"

Z shivered. "I hate those things."

Boxer Boy pulled on some jeans and took a black T-shirt from the drawer. "So who are you talking to?" he asked again. "What's with all the secrecy?"

"Okay, okay," Z said. "It's a magic trick I'm working on. For that competition."

His brother slipped on his shirt, then looked at Z. "What competition?"

"The one I've been talking about for three whole weeks. I can't believe you don't remember. Houston? The convention? That's why I go to Conjuring Cats every day." He was frustrated. He knew his family never paid attention to him, but this was major. Not knowing about his magic was like

165

not knowing he had brown hair or that their house was in Victoria, Texas.

"Hey, snap out of it," Boxer Boy said. He danced around and threw a fake punch. Then he patted Z's back. "I'm just messing with you, li'l bro. Of course I know you like magic. I just didn't think you were serious about that competition."

Z clenched his fist. If Pierre were alive, he'd be gasping for air. "I'm *totally* serious."

"Okay, man. Don't get your panties in a twist."

"I don't wear panties!"

His brother laughed. "I'm messing with you again. Can't you take a joke?"

Z glared at him and secretly vowed to take jujitsu lessons so he could get this clown in a rear naked choke next time he messed around.

His brother sat on the edge of the bed and began putting on his shoes. "Seriously," he said, "I think the competition's a great idea. I bet you'll win the whole thing."

Z lightened up, even loosened his grip on Pierre, but he still felt suspicious. "Really?"

"Sure."

"How would you know? You haven't seen me do anything."

"No one spends that much time at a magic shop without rning *something*."

Z nodded. Maybe Boxer Boy was cool after all. "So can I show you what I've been working on?" he asked.

"Sure," his brother replied, but when Z cleared his throat and held out Pierre, his brother interrupted. "You mean right now?"

Z closed his hand again. He was definitely stopping by the jujitsu gym and asking for lessons.

"Forget it," he said, stomping out.

Z headed to the living room, where his sisters were watching a cooking show. They always watched TV, and normally, he didn't care. But since he was in a bad mood, he found that he *did* care today. The way they talked *during* the show really bugged him. Besides, why did *they* get to control the TV all the time? Especially when they weren't paying attention. Without saying a word, he grabbed the remote and switched the channel, thinking they wouldn't notice, but they did.

"Hey! What's up with you?" Bossy asked as she snatched back the remote and returned to the cooking show.

Z didn't answer. Instead, he bounced Pierre a few times.

Then Boxer Boy stepped in. "I got him all mad," he said.

"Well, he changed the channel on us," Bossy said, "so we missed the most important ingredient for crêpes soufflé mariposa." Z wondered if that was a French dish and if he could sneak it into his routine.

"Yeah!" said Copycat. "He wouldn't act like a brat if you'd leave him alone."

"I'm not a brat!" Z said.

"Changing the channel is definitely a bratty thing to do," Bossy answered.

"And who made *you* the queen of our TV?" Z snapped back.

"That's telling her," Boxer Boy said. Z and his brother might fight all the time, but they always ganged up when the sisters were around.

"I'm the oldest person in the house," she explained. "That's what makes me the queen."

"You're not the oldest." Z glanced around, and then he called out, "Mom! Dad!" But no one came.

"Like I said, I'm the oldest in the house. The folks are out running errands, so I'm in charge of babysitting."

"You don't need to babysit me," Z said.

Smiley stood up and messed with his hair. "You are so cute," she said.

"So cute. Especially when you're mad," Copycat added.

Z hated the way they treated him like a baby when he was already twelve years old. When would they take him seriously?

Just then, his *other* brother stepped in. They called him

Toenail because once, when they were a lot younger, he got his toe stuck in a bicycle chain and yanked it out. The nail came off at its root, and he had to get stitches. It totally freaked Z out, and even though his brother had a normal toe again, Z couldn't forget how ugly it used to look.

Toenail had been walking the dog, and he freed it from its leash as soon as they got inside. The dog went around and sniffed everyone's shoes.

"What's up?" Toenail asked.

"Z was about to show us a magic trick," Boxer Boy said.

"Ooh! Show us some magic," Copycat said as she rubbed her hands in anticipation.

"Forget it," Z replied. He looked at his sisters. "I wouldn't want to interrupt your precious cooking show." Then he looked at Boxer Boy. "And you obviously have better things to do."

"Well, I changed my plans," he answered. "First thing on my to-do list is to figure out what you were saying to that little ball in your hands." He glanced at Pierre. "That's right." He laughed. "You're totally busted. I know you were having a conversation with your imaginary friend."

"I was practicing!" Z insisted.

"Okay, then. Prove it."

Bossy muted the TV. "Everybody, take a seat," she said. "Z's going to show us something."

Because his sisters took up the whole couch, Z's brothers sat on the armrests. Even the dog joined the audience, jumping onto the couch, too. For once, Z had everyone's attention, but even though he finally had his wish, he felt nervous. He just stared at them for a few seconds.

"Well?" Bossy moved her hand in circles as if to say, "Let's get the ball rolling."

So Z cleared his throat, wiped Pierre against his shirt, and cleared his throat again. Then he held out the ball so that his family could see the little face he'd drawn. "This is Pierre," he said. "And Pierre likes to disappear." He attempted the French drop, but instead of disappearing, Pierre fell on the ground and bounced all over the floor. His siblings laughed. Z caught the ball and said, "Pierre! You were supposed to disappear." Then he deepened his voice, and in the best French accent he could manage, he made the little ball speak. "*Excusez-moi.*"

Again, Z held out the ball. "This is Pierre, my friends, and the one thing Pierre loves to do is disappear." When he tried the French drop, Pierre slipped from his hands and bounced all over the floor again. This time his siblings laughed *and* the dog barked. Z was totally messing up his routine, but he was doing it on purpose. "Pierre!" he scolded as he caught the ball. "You are making a liar out of me." The little ball lowered his face and said, "*Excusez-moi*."

"Give it up," Toenail heckled.

Z ignored him. He held the ball once again. "This is Pierre," he repeated. "And he does *not* love to disappear. Instead, he loves to bounce all over the floor." He did the French drop, and this time, the ball disappeared! Z acted surprised as he put his hands on his hips to search the floor. Everyone followed his gaze, even the dog.

"Where'd it go?" they asked. And a moment later, Smiley clapped and said, "You made it disappear!"

"Nah," Toenail said, "it's in his hands."

Z held out his hands. They were empty. He had secretly slipped the ball into his pocket when he'd put his hands on his hips.

"That's so amazing," Smiley said. "How'd you do that?"

"Yeah, how'd you do that?" Copycat repeated.

Z put his finger to his lips. "A magician never tells his secrets."

double backer—
a card that has the picture
from the back printed on
both sides; some cards
are "two-faced," meaning
they have the face of the
card printed on both sides

LOOP

LOOP DIDN'T FEEL ONE ounce of guilt when Rubén bought him stuff. As far as Loop was concerned, Rubén owed him. So when Loop saw David Blaine holding his breath in a giant tank with hundreds of GloFish, he mentioned it, thinking he'd get tickets to a David Blaine show or a big tank so he could practice holding his breath for an impossibly long time. Wouldn't that up his cool factor? And didn't he also mention that Houdini could escape from handcuffs while he was underwater? But no. Rubén completely ignored Loop's interest in magic. He heard about the trick and ignored every detail except the fish, so instead of a giant tank, he bought a ten-gallon aquarium. He even bought glow-in-the-dark gravel, a sunken ship, and a black light. Then he took Loop to PetSmart to buy the fish. Loop dragged his feet, but he had no choice after his mom yelled at him for being ungrateful when he complained that fish were lame.

Loop didn't want a pet, but if he *had* to get one, he'd get a snake. One of his teachers had a snake, and Loop thought it was cool the way it dislocated its jaw to eat a giant rat and then there was a big lump in its body as the rat was slowly being digested. If David Blaine had jumped into a pit of venomous rattlers or escaped from the deadly grasp of a boa constrictor, Rubén would have bought a snake, and Loop would have named it Jaw or Wrath or Rage. He'd be showing it to his friends and making it a part of his magic routine. But instead, he had an aquarium with zebra fish in fluorescent colors like Sunburst Orange, Starfire Red, Galactic Purple, and Electric Green. At least they weren't guppies. *His* fish actually glowed in the dark, which was kinda cool, and since they were made in a science lab, Loop called them Frankenfish after the book he was reading. Yup, he was still reading that dumb book.

Loop dropped a pinch of food into the aquarium and

watched the fish dart around to eat. He thought about how simple they were, how they felt hungry or startled or safe, and that was about it. They couldn't even feel bored. You had to be smart to be bored. You had to be smart to be mad, too. Plus, the fish couldn't talk, which meant they couldn't lie or be lied *to*.

His grandma had a saying: *"El silencio es oro"*—silence is golden. Loop totally agreed. That's why he kept thinking about Ariel's idea, how you didn't need patter for magic because you could tell a wordless story, and it'd be pure and true. Didn't people believe that actions spoke louder than words?

So he was going to do a French drop routine without patter. Sure, he was ignoring Mr. Garza's instructions, but didn't Mr. Garza say that a magician had to act natural? For Loop, ignoring his teacher was *totally* natural.

Time to get to work, he said to himself.

He placed a large metal bolt on the floor. Then he hooked his iPod to a speaker and selected his "robo-tunes" mix, electronic music heavy on bass and synthesizers. He tapped his foot to catch the beat. Once he found it, he straightened his shoulders and lifted his arms in a classic Frankenstein's monster pose. He did a series of stiff robotic moves. Then he tilted his head to the floor and spotted the silver bolt. He picked it up, moving like a G.I. Joe action figure, stiffly bending his knees, hips, and elbows. Loop put the bolt to his nose and sniffed, then to his ear and listened, and finally into his mouth. He gulped it down and stuck out his tongue to prove he'd actually swallowed it. Then he paused a few seconds. His eyes got wide as he started to gag and choke. Finally, he covered his mouth and coughed out the bolt. He examined it, and then used the French drop to make it disappear.

Before he could go on, he heard clapping. His grandma had opened the door to spy on him, completely ignoring his crime scene tape.

She pulled the tape free, stepped into the room, and held out her arms for a hug. Loop tried to pat her on the back instead, but she grabbed him and squeezed. Then she held his face in her hands and called him *chulo*.

"I'm so glad you're still alive," she said, her voice playful. "I almost gave you CPR when I saw you choking, but I was waiting for you to turn blue first."

Loop rolled his eyes. Then he went to his iPod and turned it off.

"I should have used the Heimlich maneuver."

"Grandma," he said, all bothered by how corny she could be, "I didn't *really* have the bolt in my mouth."

"Well, you sure had *me* fooled." She grabbed his hands. Today he had outlined the veins on his arms and the lifelines on his palms. "Why do you do this?" she asked.

He shrugged. "I like drawing."

"You should draw on paper, then—not on your skin."

"I do," Loop said, grabbing his sketchpad. "I'm illustrating a book. Check it out."

His grandma flipped through the pages. The first showed a ship stuck in ice. The second had a cartoon strip. In the first picture, a man—he was all bandaged up—spoke to the captain. His speech bubble said, "I'm Dr. Frankenstein, and I had a very happy childhood." The next pictures showed Frankenstein playing with other children, then reading a book by Cornelius Agrippa, and then holding hands with a pretty girl. The third page had another cartoon strip opening with a speech bubble that said, "I loved science more than anything." The pictures that followed showed Frankenstein facing away from his family as he read books, then setting up a lab, then putting a zombie-like man on an examination table, and finally, Frankenstein holding a box with a button that said "on."

"It's from this book," Loop said, holding up his copy of *Frankenstein*. "Mom's making me read it for punishment."

"Reading? A punishment? Sounds like fun to me. I *love* books, and so should you."

"Grandma," Loop said as if talking to a five-year-old, "I'm from the twenty-first century. The only reason *you* like books is because you didn't have TV or video games when you were growing up."

She punched him. "I had TV."

"And video games?"

"Maybe I didn't have video games when I was a kid, but I *did* play them when they first came out. Ever heard of PONG?"

Loop moaned. And then he felt sorry for his grandma because PONG was the lamest video game on the planet. There were no graphics, unless you counted a black screen with two white bars and a little white dot. The whole point of the game was to move the bars up and down to hit the dot. No background music or avatars or world building. No wonder she liked books.

"Trust me, Grandma," Loop said. "If you had Minecraft when you were growing up, you wouldn't waste your time reading."

She sighed. "My poor, lost child." Then she reached into her bag and pulled out a Sacred Heart of Jesus candle. "You know what we need to do?"

Loop moaned again.

"That's right," she said. "We need to pray for your soul."

Loop glanced at his GloFish. Lucky things. No one asked *them* to pray.

He put on his altar-boy face, but he was pretending. Sure, he liked God, Jesus, and La Virgen de Guadalupe, but he didn't like to pray. He'd rather choke on a bolt for *real* and get mouth-to-mouth resuscitation from his grandma, no matter how gross it was. That's why he felt like a double backer, or a two-faced gaff card, with the same thing printed on both sides. They fooled you because you thought they were normal cards, but instead, they were total fakes.

His grandma grabbed two pillows and placed them before the *retablo*. She dusted the little statue of Mary and made room for the candle. Then she lit it and knelt down.

"Come on," she said to Loop, pulling on his arm.

He plopped down next to her. "I never know what to say after the Our Father and Hail Mary."

"Just have a conversation," she suggested.

"About what? I mean, what do *you* talk about?"

"Well." His grandma paused a moment. "First I give gratitude for all the good things in my life—like my family and friends, and all the times we're safe, and for the food on the table and good weather, and beautiful things like rivers and roses. Then I make petitions so I can ask for help. I always need help. Like with my doctor's appointments. And the people I love need help, too, so I pray for them, hoping they forgive each other no matter how mad they are." At that, she looked directly at Loop. He got the hint. She wanted him to forgive his mom and Rubén, but it wasn't that easy.

He shrugged it off. No need to get his grandma upset. "Say thanks and ask for things?" he said. "That's all I gotta do?"

She nodded. Then she turned to the *retablo* and made the sign of the cross. Loop made the sign of the cross, too . . . only his looked more like a squiggle. He took a deep breath before rushing through the prayers, his "Our Father, who art in heaven" turning into "Are there warts in heav'n?" Then it was time to give thanks.

"Okay, God," he said, but not out loud, "thanks for the GloFish, even though I didn't ask for them. I guess they're your creatures, too. So what do you think about scientists injecting them with jellyfish genes so they'll glow in the dark?" He paused a moment as if listening to the answer. "And thanks for the chop cup," he went on. "I'll be able to do some cool tricks with that. And for the liquid latex so I could make some fake skin." At this point, he made a mental note: *Get chop cup from Dominic before he thinks it's his. And Z still has the Svengali deck. They need to buy their own magic stuff from now on, especially after hightailing it yesterday and leaving me to walk home alone.*

Thinking about all the things he had lent his friends made Loop lose his concentration, so he glanced at the ceiling, wondering what else to be grateful for. When he couldn't think of anything, he switched to making petitions. His grandma said you shouldn't ask for objects, since that was being materialistic. Instead, you should ask for ways to improve your life.

But how could he improve his life when all his mistakes had already happened? It wasn't like he could fix them by time traveling to the past. Of course, winning the magic contest would improve his life. Maybe you didn't win money, but you could win respect. Everyone thought he was a slacker. If he won, he could prove them wrong, but that wasn't going to happen when his friends took his props all the time.

Loop suddenly knew what to ask for. He decided to chat with La Virgen de Guadalupe, thinking it would be easier to persuade her since they shared the same name. "Okay, O.G., I need help," he began quietly. "I got these friends who are giving me grief. Seriously. They don't have resources, so they come to me. And I'm supposed to buy them stuff. Now, before you think I'm selfish, let me remind you that I'm more than happy to spare some change for snow cones and movie tickets. I don't mind letting them download playlists, either. But I'm supposed to sponsor them for the magic convention, too? That'd be like Batman lending his Batmobile to the Joker. How does that make sense? It's like *paying* the competition to defeat you." He stopped, realizing he hadn't made his petition yet. "So here's the deal, O.G. I'm not asking you to give them money, because that would be materialistic. But maybe you could help them accept their situations. That way, they'll stop bugging me for stuff. Sometimes, they're as annoying as hard snot in the nose." He flinched. "Wait. I take that back. Please forgive me for saying my friends are like snot." He stared at the little statue. She had such a pleasant smile. "Really, I don't want anything for myself. Just make it so my buddies stop caring about that competition, since they probably won't get enough money to go anyway. Think about how happy they'll be when they accept that they're staying behind."

This was the most reasonable, selfless petition he had ever made. He wanted to pat himself on the back or shake his own hand, but he didn't think his grandma would approve. He waited a moment in case he got another great idea. He didn't, so he said, "Amen," this time out loud.

A few seconds later, his grandma said, "Amen," too. And then she said, "I always feel better after I pray."

Loop put his hand on her shoulder and smiled. "Me too."

burn—
when spectators closely
watch magicians in
order to catch their
sleights of hand

LOOP

AFTER HIS GRANDMA LEFT, Loop decided to contact his friends to ask them to return his magic stuff. First, he texted Dominic.

Loop: need chop cup bck
Dominic: ?
Loop: don't play dumb
Dominic: u gave it 2 me
Loop: lent it
Dominic: 2 bad. mine now

Loop: give it bck

Dominic: u don't even use it

Loop: u don't either

Dominic: whatever . . . it's at shop

Loop: it better be

Next, he contacted Z to ask for his Svengali deck, but since Z wasn't at home and didn't have a cell phone, Loop had to leave a message.

He decided to cover all his bases by calling Conjuring Cats. When Ariel answered, he said, "Did Dominic leave a chop cup there?"

She took a minute to reply, probably because she was looking for it.

"Yeah, there's a chop cup here. Why?"

"It's mine. I let him borrow it, but now I need it back. Are the balls there, too?"

"It's all here, but . . ." Her voice trailed off.

"But what?"

"I'm not sure I should say this because I don't want to cause any trouble, but the last time I saw Dominic with the chop cup, he was doing something weird."

"Like what?"

Ariel hesitated. "Well..."

"Well, *what*?" Loop started pacing. "Tell me," he demanded.

"Dominic had a bunch of magnets," Ariel said. "Different sizes. He kept putting them against the chop cup. When I asked him what he was doing, he said he was conducting an experiment."

"An experiment? Like for science?"

"That's what he said. And then he told me he loves reading, especially science books. So, yeah, he did a science experiment on your chop cup."

"He's a total geek sometimes," Loop said. "Is the chop cup okay? He didn't melt it or anything, did he?"

"It looks normal to me," Ariel said. Then, when Loop did not reply, "Anything else?" she asked. "I'm kind of busy over here."

"If you see Z, make sure he leaves my Svengali deck. I bet he doesn't want to give it back, but it's my property. I bought it with my own money."

"Sure," she said. "Svengali deck."

"Thanks. I'll come by next week to pick up my stuff."

"Suit yourself," she said.

Loop was so annoyed. The number one rule when you

borrowed something was to take care of it. If Loop were to borrow something from his friends, like a book, he would not dog-ear the pages, write notes in the margins, or break the spines. He wouldn't even drink hot chocolate while reading because it might spill on the page. He'd wash his hands before touching it, too. He would *not* use the book for his own experiments. And he wouldn't borrow the book if he had money to buy his own copy.

This was the last time his friends were taking advantage of him. He was *never* going to lend them anything again! And every time they got near his stuff, he was going to watch them closely, just like spectators who burn magicians because they don't want to be fooled by the magic act.

repertoire—
a list of tricks that a
magician is able to
perform

WHY DID LOOP WANT the chop cup all of a sudden? Sure, Dominic had borrowed it, but only to see how it worked. And the reason he wanted to figure it out was to show Loop and Z. It wasn't like *they* would ever solve the gimmick.

Loop doesn't really want it back, Dominic realized. *He's just getting back at me for what I said about his dad the other day.*

"If that's how he wants to play it," Dominic mumbled to himself, "he can have the chop cup. But no way is he getting the quarter shell. He *gave* that to me."

He looked up the number for Conjuring Cats and dialed, noticing that he'd missed several calls from his mom. He'd check the messages later.

"Conjuring Cats. This is Ariel speaking." She sounded so professional. Her whole voice had changed. Instead of someone in middle school, she sounded like someone in college.

"Hi, Ariel. It's Dominic."

That's when he heard smacking. She must have been chewing gum. "We got, like, ten minutes before we close," she said, all annoyed. "You have some magic emergency or what?" She was the normal version of herself again, and Dominic couldn't help smiling, even if this was the rude side of her personality.

"Did I leave my quarter shell there?" he asked.

Except for the smacking, she was silent on the other end.

"Did you hear me?"

"Yes, I heard you. It's just that..." She left a giant fill-in-the-blank at the end of her sentence.

"It's just what?" Dominic asked.

"I didn't know it was *your* quarter shell. I thought it belonged to Z because he was using it today."

"He was? Why? He doesn't do coin magic. He likes cards."

"That's what I thought at first. And then I figured he wanted to expand his repertoire or something. Anyway, he left it here, so I guess it *does* belong to you. You can pick it up tomorrow." She paused and stopped chewing her gum. Then she used her professional voice again. "We're open Tuesday through Saturday from ten in the morning to seven in the evening."

"I know your hours," Dominic said, "but I'm out of town for the next two weeks. Do you think you can mail it to me if I give you my dad's address?"

Ariel sighed—loudly. Dominic knew that he was bothering her and that she had better things to do, but he gave her his address anyway.

When they disconnected, he decided to check his voice mail. His mom had left five messages! What was wrong with her? He'd been gone only two days.

Dominic shook his head. His mom was too overprotective, and it really bugged him sometimes. He couldn't take three steps out of the apartment without telling her where he was going. Why couldn't she relax and be more like his dad? He really didn't want to talk to her right now, so he decided to call back later.

escape artist—
a performer who
specializes in freeing
himself from constraints
like handcuffs,
straitjackets, and
locked boxes

A FEW DAYS LATER, Z and his siblings argued about which channel to watch while their parents ran errands. They'd been running errands for three days in a row. Z wondered what they were up to, but every time he asked, they said, "It's a surprise."

"No more cooking shows!" Boxer Boy shouted as he snatched the remote from Copycat. "You don't even cook."

"Well, no more boxing or UFC," she snapped back.

Since they were yelling so loud, no one heard the honking at first. Finally, Bossy went, "Shh!" and everyone got quiet. "What's that noise?" she said as she went to the door and opened it. There was a lot more honking, so the whole family followed. When they stepped outside, they spotted an extra car in the driveway—a white Toyota Camry. Z's dad stepped out of his Ford F-150 truck, and Z's mom stepped out of the new car.

"Look what we bought!" she said, opening the doors, the hood, and the trunk so everyone could take a peek.

Z's brothers and sisters cheered as they ran to the new car. They inspected the engine, the tires, and the seats. They started fighting over the keys. Their parents explained that the car was for everyone, that they'd have to work out a schedule because from now on, the kids were going to have to drive one another to work and school.

Z should have been excited, too, but he could only think about how much money the car cost. And how did a new car help *him*? He didn't have a driver's license. He went everywhere on his skateboard or bike. And the biggest question was...now that his parents had car payments, how were they going to pay for the magic convention?

He went inside and picked up the phone. His friends had really upset him last week, but living in a house with a bunch of brothers and sisters had taught him that holding grudges got you nowhere. Best to forgive and forget. So first he called Dominic. But there was no answer. *He probably hit "ignore" on his phone*, Z thought. *At least I have Loop.* He dialed the number, but Loop's mom picked up the phone. "He can't talk right now," she said. "He's reading."

Why would Loop be reading? He hated books. With one friend ignoring him and the other making up an excuse, Z got mad. What had happened to being buddies through thick and thin? And why were they mad at *him*? He hadn't done anything wrong. As far as he was concerned, *they* should be begging *him* for forgiveness.

He was about to look up the number for Conjuring Cats—maybe Ariel would listen—but then he heard an engine start. He peeked out and saw his siblings squeezed into the Camry, the dog sticking its head out the window, and Bossy in the driver's seat. They were going for a ride, and once again, they'd forgotten to include him.

"Figures," he mumbled. "I'm just invisible to them."

Just then, his parents stepped in, surprised to see him.

"*¿Qué pasó?*" his dad said. "Why are you in here by yourself?"

"Don't you want to go for a ride?" his mom asked.

Z shook his head. He wanted to cry—that's how frustrated he felt—but there was no way he was going to let the tears out.

"Aren't you excited about the car?" his mom asked.

Z shook his head again.

His dad put a hand on Z's shoulder. "What is it, *mijo*?"

Z looked at his parents. With everyone gone and the TV still on mute, the house was amazingly quiet.

"Why would I care about the car?" he said. "I can't even drive. And you know no one's going to give me a ride anywhere. They'll tell me to take my bike."

"You'll be driving in a few years," his dad said.

"Sure. By then, the car will be all messed up. *Everything* I get is messed up." He held out the hem of his T-shirt to show them a little hole. "This was here by the time I got this shirt. It's like that with all my clothes because they always belong to someone else first."

"You want some new clothes?" his mom asked, as if he were a giant puzzle to solve.

"No." Z took a deep breath. "I don't care about that."

"Then what is it?"

"I never ask for anything," he said. "Not really. But now I *am* asking for something."

198

His parents stared at him, waiting for an explanation.

"I want to go to that magic convention and compete in the close-up contest."

His parents glanced at each other. He could tell they'd already discussed this.

"It costs a lot of money," his father said. "We want you to go, but a magic convention is not something"—he paused—"that's for *everyone*."

Z's mom jumped in. "Like the car," she explained. "It's for the whole family. But this contest is only for you, and as much as we love you, *mijo*, we have to do what's best for *everybody*."

"But..." Z couldn't finish his sentence. Instead, he reached into his pocket for Pierre and threw him hard against the floor. He let Pierre's bounces get smaller and smaller until finally the ball rolled under the couch. "I'm always last," he told his parents, "so nothing is ever best for *me*." He rushed to his room because holding back tears was getting tough, and the last thing he wanted was to cry in front of people. If he did, he'd never get rid of his baby-of-the-family status.

Once in his room, he started cleaning. He even picked up his brothers' stuff, just to forget about being upset. He kept thinking of escape artists like Houdini. They could get out of any situation—even being tied up, handcuffed, locked in a box, and dumped underwater! If only Z could escape, too. Maybe, somewhere, he'd find a family who wouldn't forget about him or push him aside all the time.

As he tried to calm down, he heard his parents talking. He couldn't make out their words, but he knew they were speaking about him. After a while, they stepped into the room, the registration form in their hands.

"We signed it," his dad said. "It says you can pay when you get to the convention."

"We can give you some money to help, but you'll have to find a way to earn the rest," his mother said.

"Maybe you can mow some lawns," his dad suggested.

"Or wash some cars," his mom added.

His dad reached out and put an arm around Z. "We wish we had more, *mijo*. But business has been slow, and we have to make sure we put money aside in case it doesn't pick up again. Understand?"

Z nodded as he looked at the form. Sure enough, they had signed it, and sure enough, the payment was due on the first day of the convention. "Thanks," he said as he threw his arms around them. Maybe he didn't have the money yet, but at least he had their support.

geek magic—
tricks that are
designed to shock the
audience

LOOP

LOOP'S MOM WOULDN'T LET him talk to his friends or go to Conjuring Cats until he read at least one more chapter of *Frankenstein*. So he forced himself to read, and when he finally finished that chapter, he went to give her an update on the book.

"Dr. Frankenstein is a wimp," Loop reported. "He spends all this time gathering body parts and then using electricity to jolt the thing alive, and when he succeeds, he freaks out because it looks like a zombie. What did he expect? You can't be surprised when your project looks messed up because you mixed a bunch of parts. That's like building a car from motorcycles, trucks, and minivans. You're going to end up with one ugly machine. But, hey, if it works, who cares? That's the whole point of a car, right? To get from one place to another? And the whole point of Dr. Frankenstein's experiment was to see if he could make something dead come back to life. He totally did that, so I don't see why he ran off screaming."

Loop's mother thought for a moment. "Perhaps he ran off because he hadn't considered the true consequences of his actions."

"He *totally* considered the consequences. He wanted to make something dead come alive, and he did that."

"I mean the *next* set of consequences."

Loop got a little confused. "What next set of consequences?"

"Like whether the experiment was the right thing to do. Sometimes, just because you *can* do something doesn't mean you *should*. Every time a scientist thinks of a new experiment, he has to consider whether it will do more harm than good."

Loop considered this. "Like the Manhattan Project and the atomic bomb?"

"Exactly. Wow! I'm surprised you know about that."

"I'm not a moron," Loop said. "I know lots of stuff, and I don't need straight As to prove it."

Loop knew about the Manhattan Project because of a show on the History Channel. In addition to sports, he and Rubén used to watch documentaries. That's how he learned that the Manhattan Project was when a bunch of scientists got together to create the first atomic bomb. The bomb was used against Japan in World War II, and it basically ended the war. Even though the scientists were happy about this, they felt awful about creating something that could kill so many people. The most horrible part was what happened to the people who survived the bomb. They got radiation poisoning, which was like being cooked from the inside out. Talk about some serious consequences.

Loop remembered how he and Rubén had stayed up for hours talking about the bomb. They had gone online to learn more, and the best part was knowing there wasn't going to be a test afterward. Rubén didn't even quiz him. Believe it or not, Loop remembered more when he didn't have tests or quizzes or "updates." But try explaining *that* to his teachers and his mom.

Loop's shoulders dropped a bit, and his mom noticed. "What's wrong?" she asked.

"Nothing," Loop said, because he didn't want to admit

that he missed watching TV with Rubén. Sure, Rubén invited him every time something interesting came on, but Loop always said no.

His mom was satisfied with his report, so he rode his skateboard to Conjuring Cats. After saying hello to Mrs. Garza and petting Diamonds and Spades, he went into the Vault.

Mr. Garza sat at the computer as usual, but Ariel wasn't around.

"She's at the movies with some friends," Mr. Garza explained.

This surprised Loop. He didn't know Ariel had friends or even watched movies. In fact, he couldn't imagine her outside of Conjuring Cats, the same way he couldn't imagine his teachers outside of their classrooms. Certain people, it seemed, existed in specific places, and it was hard to remember that they existed in other places, too.

Mr. Garza turned away from his computer. He was wearing his ASSASSIN'S BREED T-shirt again. "Have you come up with an idea for your routine?"

Loop explained that he liked geek magic because he wanted to freak people out. "I'm not going to put a sword through my neck or swallow razor blades," he explained.

"Instead, I'm going to do one of Criss Angel's tricks." Criss Angel was Loop's favorite geek magician. "I've been studying his YouTube videos and practicing his techniques. I'm even getting an outfit so I can look just like him."

"Hmmm…" Mr. Garza said. He did a full 360 in his chair before continuing. "I'm glad you found a magician you admire. It's a good idea to model your heroes, especially when you're in your development stage, but if you want to win the contest, you have to come up with your own routine. ¿*Entiendes?*"

Loop shook his head because he *didn't* understand. "How can I come up with my own routine? I don't know enough."

Mr. Garza thought a moment. "Have you ever used odds and ends to make something?"

"No," Loop replied, thinking about how Dr. Frankenstein had used odds and ends to make a monster.

"Have you ever made a collage using pictures from different magazines?"

"No."

"How about cooking? Have you ever cooked anything?"

"No."

"Well, what do you do?" Mr. Garza asked. "Besides magic, that is."

Loop took a deep breath and stared at the ceiling for a while. He didn't do anything except play video games, read *Frankenstein*, and draw pictures. So that's what he said.

"What kind of pictures?" Mr. Garza wanted to know.

"Right now, I'm drawing comic strips about the book. I don't really want to. My mom's making me do it because I got bad grades in school."

"Are your comic strips a direct copy of someone else's?"

"No. That would be plagiarism." Loop stopped himself because he didn't want Mr. Garza to know that he had plagiarized an important paper once and that his teacher had sent him to in-school suspension *and* had a conference with his parents.

"So what you're doing," Mr. Garza went on, "is taking elements from the book and examples of comics, and combining them to create something new."

Loop nodded. "I think I get it," he said. "Instead of copying Criss Angel, you want me to take a few *elements* from his acts and maybe a few elements from something else, like video games or the *Frankenstein* book, and blend them together."

"That's right. And remember, above all..."

"...be natural," Loop said to complete the sentence.

"Exactly."

Loop thought for a moment. "This is going to be tough," he admitted.

"You're a smart young man. I'm sure you'll figure it out."

With that, Mr. Garza turned back to his computer. Meanwhile, Loop had a giant smile on his face. Mr. Garza didn't know Loop as a student in school. He knew him only as a student at Conjuring Cats. That meant that Mr. Garza knew the *real* Loop. *And I am smart*, Loop thought to himself. *I'm going to prove it, too.*

He found a memo pad and a pencil so he could brainstorm. Every time he heard that word—"brainstorm"—he imagined lightning and thunder inside himself, so Loop sketched an outline of his head with a storm inside. He could almost feel the booms of thunder and the jolts of electric lightning. In a way, brainstorming was what happened when Dr. Frankenstein flipped the switch on his monster, so Loop sketched Dr. Frankenstein's monster, even though it had nothing to do with his magic routine. He was just letting his mind wander. Next, it wandered over to Criss Angel, and Loop drew him with his long black hair and clunky silver crosses. Then Loop wrote a list of all of Criss Angel's tricks. He drew boxes around some and then arrows to mark the starting points of other lists. He wrote down props and sleights, underlining some and crossing out others. He flipped pages when he ran out of space. Finally, he drew a circle and wrote "other non-magic details," and then he drew spokes coming out from the circle. One said "costume," another said "makeup," and a third said "sound effects." He drew circles around these words and more spokes with more words, and on and on until he ran out of pages. And then he shook out his hand because he had never written so much in one hour.

Loop stretched and yawned. That's how tired he was.

"I've got a few ideas," he announced. "This is going to be the awesomest routine in the world."

"I have no doubt," Mr. Garza said.

Loop was ready to go, so he grabbed the memo pad and the chop cup, which was on the counter just like Ariel had said. He put these items in a plastic bag and headed home. When he got to his room, he reviewed his notes. Little by little, a routine was forming in his mind. He couldn't wait to start working on it. In the meantime, he decided to mess around with the chop cup, but when he picked it up, he noticed something weird. The little balls weren't disappearing like they were supposed to. He double-checked his process. He was doing everything right, but still, the balls wouldn't disappear!

And then he remembered Dominic's experiment—Dominic must have broken the gimmick. This was deliberate sabotage!

Loop thought about his conversation with his mother earlier, about the true consequences of experiments. Well, here was a true consequence for Dominic. Not only had he ruined the chop cup, but he had also ruined their friendship!

Ambitious Card—
a trick featuring a
card that continually
rises to the top of
the deck

Z SPENT A WHOLE week looking for jobs. "I'll clean your room," he told his brothers, and they said, "Nice try, it's your room, too." To his sisters, he tried, "I'll wash your clothes," but they said, "We don't want you touching our underwear."

So he went around the neighborhood with the lawn mower, but since it hadn't rained, the yards were all dried up. Only Mr. Crane's yard had grass because he ignored the water restrictions and used the sprinkler every morning. But Z couldn't mow his lawn because Mr. Crane did it himself.

"I don't know what to do," he complained after another day of failing to find a job.

His oldest brothers and sisters had jobs at fast-food places or clothing stores, but Boxer Boy and Copycat didn't work. Like Z, they helped around the house without getting paid. Right now, Boxer Boy was outside giving the dog a bath, and Copycat was washing dishes while their mom ironed clothes.

"There's a lot to do here," his sister said. "You want to wash these dishes for me?"

"Are you going to pay me?"

She laughed. "Very funny," she said.

He plopped on the couch. "I'm never going to make enough money for the magic convention."

"Speaking of magic," his mom said, "your friend Loop left a message last week. I'm sorry I forgot to tell you before. He said something about a deck of cards. A spaghetti deck or something?"

"You mean 'Svengali'?"

She shrugged.

"What else did he say?"

"He wants it back."

This surprised Z because Loop never did card tricks.

214

"Are you sure? He hates messing around with cards. Besides, he has all kinds of magic tricks because his parents can afford to buy him anything he wants. He doesn't have to share everything with a bunch of brothers and sisters."

His mom gave him a stern look. "You should be grateful for your brothers and sisters," she said.

"Yeah," Copycat said. "Aren't you grateful for me?" She curtsied.

Z ignored her. "So far," he went on, "I've made exactly zero dollars and zero cents. This is definite proof that I'm cursed. Loop has the messiest room, but he still gets an allowance just because he was born. He doesn't have to lift a finger, and his parents *still* give him money."

"And what about your other friend?" his sister asked. "Does he get money just because he was born?"

"No, he does chores."

"*Qué bueno*," his mom said.

"But he gets *paid* when he does chores. Shouldn't I get *something* for helping out? I swept the driveway yesterday, and all Dad gave me was a glass of water. Then he told me to sweep the back patio. I feel like a slave sometimes!"

His mother held up the iron. It looked like she wanted to brand him. "Around here," she said, "we work because it's our responsibility to help one another. We don't do it for money. Besides, you get an allowance when we have a little extra."

"That's right," his sister added. "I'm not getting a cent for washing these dishes today."

"But—"

Before Z could finish, his mom said, "Go do chores at your friend's house if you want to get paid." With that, she pressed the iron hard against some slacks, and steam rose from it, making the iron seem as angry as she was. For a minute, Z felt guilty about upsetting her, but then he realized that she had just made a great suggestion.

He jumped from the couch and kissed her on the cheek. "You're a genius!" he said. "Dominic's out of town, so there's no one to help his mom!"

He ran out the door and raced to the apartment complex. When Dominic's mom answered the door, she said, "I'm afraid Dominic's not back yet. He's staying one more week at his father's house."

"That's okay," Z said. "I'm not here to see him. I'm here to see you."

"Really?" she said. "Well, that's wonderful. I was getting lonely all by myself." She let him in, and Z took a seat on the couch. Then she asked if he wanted some milk and cookies. He said yes, so she went to the kitchen for his snack. Z finished the cookies and milk in less than a minute. With his giant family, he had to rush through meals if he wanted seconds, so he was used to eating fast.

"These are so delicious," he said, his mouth still full.

Dominic's mom smiled. "I'm glad you enjoyed them. Now, what brings you to the apartment?"

Z told her the whole story—how his parents were running out of money because business was slow and they had too many kids and how his brothers and sisters ignored him because he was the youngest and how he was always last so there was never anything left for him. "That's why I have to compete in that magic contest," he explained. "I know I can win, because I'm really good at every card trick that has ever been invented. My parents said I can go, but only if I raise some money. Even though they're broke, they went and bought a car for all my brothers and sisters, but not for me, since I can't drive yet. So all I get is a *little* bit of money. See what I mean?" He didn't wait for an answer. "I've been all over the place looking for lawns to mow or cars to wash, but I'm not having any luck. So then I thought about you and how you're by yourself this week. Maybe I can take over Dominic's chores while he's gone, and you can give me his allowance."

She thought a moment and then said, "You're an enterprising young man, Z."

He didn't know what "enterprising" meant, but it sounded like a compliment, so he said, "Thanks!"

"I'm more than happy to give you some money in exchange for help this week, but I'm afraid it won't be enough to cover the whole convention."

"I know," Z said. "I'll need to bug a lot of people to give me jobs."

"I'm glad to hear about your perseverance in spite of all the obstacles."

Perseverance? With all this vocabulary, Z thought, *no wonder Dominic is smart.*

"I have a lot of friends around the apartment complex," she continued. "I'll see if anyone else needs help. In the meantime, I was about to wash clothes. Maybe you can help me carry the baskets and wait for the loads to finish. I don't like to leave them unattended because once someone stole my towels straight from the dryer. I know it sounds boring, but you can read one of Dominic's books while you wait."

"Thanks, but I've got cards." Z showed them to her. "I'll practice while I wait."

"Excellent way to multitask," she said.

Z helped Dominic's mom take the baskets to the laundry room, which was right by a swimming pool. She loaded the machines and showed him how to work the dryers and which settings she preferred. Then she left him alone to wait.

He was all by himself, but that was okay. He played a little game with his cards, lifting some and guessing how many were in his hand without spreading them out. He had a special talent for it.

He'd watched dozens of YouTube videos and couldn't believe how many tricks could be done with a simple deck of cards. But one trick interested him more than the others. It was called the Ambitious Card. Z liked it because he was ambitious, too.

When the clothes finished, Dominic's mom gave Z five dollars and told him to come back the next day to help her friends. Then she handed him a ziplock bag with extra cookies. "For later," she said. Z beamed. The cookies would be his secret. He wasn't going to share them with *anyone*—especially not his brothers and sisters.

prediction—
when a magician guesses
what the audience is
going to say or choose

DOMINIC HAD BEEN IN Corpus for a whole week, and he'd spent most of his time practicing magic. Luckily, his dad was 100 percent supportive. He took Dominic to a local magic shop, and even though Dominic felt guilty about not buying from Conjuring Cats, he couldn't resist a new mentalism trick called Die-ception. It used a die—not the small kind that came with board games, but a four-inch cube. According to the instructions, you asked people to choose a number, and then you guessed it even when it was hidden inside a cloth sack. Dominic figured out how it worked. It was actually easy. The *real* challenge was writing patter.

He took the prediction die and a notepad to the dining table, and he brainstormed all morning, finally coming up with patter for the trick—and this time, he wasn't going to talk about the evaporation cycle. Now all he had to do was practice. Little by little, using patter while performing his tricks got easier and easier, so as soon as his dad came home from work, Dominic asked if he wanted to see what he'd come up with.

"You bet," his dad said. He had the mail in his hand, so he placed it on the table and took a seat.

Then Dominic had a great idea. When he'd finally called his mom back last week, she made him promise to touch base every day, even if only with a text message. Perhaps he could touch base right now, while he was performing his new trick. "Mom's home from work," he told his dad. "Why don't we Skype her, so she can see the trick, too?" His dad seemed to hesitate. "You don't have to talk to her. But it'll be like both of you being in the same place at the same time." He got no response from his dad. "For the trick," Dominic added.

"Well, son," his dad finally said. "Your mom's probably

tired. Why don't you show her your trick later? That way, she can have you all to herself."

Dominic wanted to say that she *always* had him to herself, but he knew it was pointless. He decided to shrug it off and get to his routine. He took a deep breath, cleared his throat, and took a deep breath again. He desperately needed to calm down because he was getting anxious.

"This here," he said, "is a regular die. See for yourself." His dad looked at it, examining all the sides. "I'm going to turn away," Dominic went on, "and while my back is turned, I want you to choose a number on the die. Place the die on the table with the number facing up and then cover it with this handkerchief." He caught his father nodding as he turned away.

A few seconds passed. "Okay," his dad said. "I picked a number and covered it up."

Dominic turned around. "Don't tell me what it is," he warned. "I'm going to read your mind. Are you ready?"

His father nodded.

"Now concentrate really hard as you think of the number." He squinted his eyes. "Wait a minute," he said, "concentrate on the die, not on the number pi."

He thought the rhyme was funny, but his dad didn't laugh.

Dominic continued. He closed his eyes and touched his father's head. "You sure have a lot of numbers in there—credit card accounts, math equations, the number of miles on your car—but one number keeps rising to the top. It's getting bigger and bigger. It's flashing red now. This has to be it!" He opened his eyes. "You picked the number four."

His dad clapped. "That's exactly right!" he said as Dominic lifted the handkerchief and revealed the four.

"Maybe you think I cheated," Dominic went on. "Maybe you think this handkerchief is see-through. Let's try this again, but this time put the die in this sack. Make sure the number you choose is facing up and then close the sack. I won't be able to see what you picked because the bag's made of impenetrable fabric. See for yourself." His dad examined the bag. "This bag is as thick as a telephone book."

His simile got no reaction.

"Okay," Dominic said. "I'm going to turn around again. Go ahead and pick a number and put the die in the bag."

He turned and heard shuffling sounds, and then his dad said, "I'm ready."

Dominic faced his dad again. Instead of closing his eyes, he stared not at the bag but at his father. "Cyclops," he said. "Ears. Tricycle. Square. Hand. Guitar...aha! Guitar!"

"Guitar?" his dad repeated, all confused.

"I knew you weren't going to think of the number, that you'd try to fool me, so I used an associative technique."

"An associative technique?"

"Let me put it this way. One eye on a Cyclops. Two ears on a head. Three wheels on a tricycle, four corners on a square, five fingers on a hand, and six strings on a guitar."

His dad just stared at him.

"As soon as I said 'guitar,' your mind flashed a six." He waved his hand over the bag. "You may now reveal the die."

His dad opened the sack, and the die was a six as predicted. He clapped, and Dominic took a bow.

"So what did you think?" Dominic asked.

"You're great at reading my mind. Both times you figured out the number."

"But was I funny?"

"Well, son." His dad leaned back and took a deep breath. "Being funny is not your thing, but that's okay. Really. You're a smart kid, and I'm proud to have a smart kid like you."

"But, Dad, did it make sense at least? Not the trick, but the stuff I said?"

"I'm sure it would make sense to *smart* people, but

your old man isn't one of them." He glanced back to make sure no one else was in the room. "You got *that* from your mother. I'm sure she'll completely understand your trick when you show it to her later."

Dominic dropped his head. He knew his dad was complimenting him by saying he was smart, but he was also saying that Dominic was boring, even if those weren't the exact words he used. Why *else* would he compare Dominic to his mom? She had a lot of great qualities, but being interesting wasn't one of them. *And it isn't one of my great qualities, either*, Dominic thought to himself.

"Cheer up," his dad said. "You can't ace everything. Maybe the die trick isn't for you." He grabbed the mail and shuffled through the envelopes, handing one to Dominic. "Look. It's for you," he said.

It was from Conjuring Cats! Dominic had been waiting the whole week. "It's my quarter shell," he announced. He ripped open the package and pulled out the quarter shell, but it was too heavy. When he turned it around, a quarter was stuck in it. He tried to take out the coin, but it wouldn't budge. Then he remembered his conversation with Ariel. She'd mentioned that Z was practicing with the quarter shell because he wanted to expand his repertoire. *But he wasn't expanding his repertoire . . .*, Dominic realized.

"What's wrong?" his father asked.

"Z glued a quarter in the shell. It's totally useless now."

"Why would he do that?"

"I don't know," Dominic said. "But as soon as I get back, I'm going to find out."

steal—
a sleight that occurs
when a magician secretly
takes an object

THE NEXT DAY, Z went right to Conjuring Cats after helping a few people at the apartment complex. He hadn't been to the store since his fight with his friends because he'd been too busy looking for work. But now that he had a job—for this week at least—he wanted to figure out his routine.

When he entered the Vault, Mr. Garza was missing, but Ariel was at a table writing in her notebook again. She hardly looked up when Z said hello.

"I need to come up with a routine," he said. "But I don't

know where to start. It's like I know how to dribble, pivot, and do a layup, but I still don't know how to play basketball. What I mean is … well … what am I supposed to do with all these sleights I've learned?"

Ariel didn't answer.

"Did you hear me?" Z asked, frustrated because he hated being ignored. "I really need a routine. I've been thinking about doing the Ambitious Card. Think I can win the contest with that?"

She put down her pen. "My father's running errands. He'll be back soon. Why don't you ask *him*?"

"That could take hours," Z said, remembering that when *his* parents ran errands, they were out for the entire day. "Why can't *you* help? You know how to do card tricks. Besides, aren't you bored doing homework all summer?"

"This is not homework," she said, glancing at her notebook. "I'm writing my memoir, if you really have to know, but I'm never going to finish with you and your friends coming here at all hours."

"My friends were here?"

"*One* of them. Loop. He was here the other day."

"All by himself?"

"Well, if he's not with you and he's not with Dominic, then, yes, he's all by himself."

"Did he mention my Svengali deck?"

Ariel shut her journal and folded her hands on top of it. "As a matter of fact, he did call about it, and according to him, it's not yours but his." Then she looked at the lockers. If her eyes were signs, they'd be flashing arrows.

Z rushed to his locker, where he had stored the Svengali deck. He had a hoodie in there from the one time it had rained. He also had a bag of potato chips, an empty water bottle, a few gaff cards, some sponge bunnies, random coupons, and a gaming magazine. But the Svengali deck? It was gone!

He took everything out of his locker. He checked and double-checked the pockets of his hoodie. He looked at the floor in case the deck had fallen out. But it was 100 percent gone!

Z slammed the locker door. He couldn't believe it. Loop had stolen the Svengali deck!

In magic, a steal was when you secretly took an object. You could steal a ball when doing a cups-and-balls routine, or you could do a side steal for certain card tricks, or if you were Apollo Robbins, you could steal watches right off your spectators' wrists. But you were not supposed to steal from your friends!

"Lose something?" Ariel asked.

"Was Loop at my locker? Did you actually *see* him take my Svengali deck?"

She shrugged. "I wasn't here earlier, so I didn't see him take anything. You'll have to ask my father. But..."

"But what?"

"Well...I hate to suggest this, but maybe you should look in *his* locker."

Z stared at Loop's locker. He didn't want to open it. After all, the reason he and his friends had not bought locks was because they trusted one another. But his deck of cards didn't have legs. It couldn't walk away by itself. *Somebody* had taken it. If he peeked in Loop's locker and did not see the deck, then he'd know Loop was innocent. This was called "eliminating a suspect" on the crime shows. But if he peeked in the locker and saw the deck, then he'd know that Loop had betrayed him. The suspense was killing him.

"Go on," Ariel said. "I won't tell him you peeked."

Z took a deep breath, and then he opened Loop's locker. There it was—the box for his Svengali deck! Then he noticed something else, too—scissors and...

"Oh no!" Z cried.

Ariel approached the locker. "What is it?" she asked.

"Loop cut up the cards! He totally ruined my Svengali deck!"

transformation—
in magic, to change the
appearance or identity
of a person or object

LOOP

LOOP HAD BEEN STUCK at home for a whole week with his boring GloFish because his mother wouldn't let him go to Conjuring Cats until he finished *Frankenstein*.

"That's going to take forever!" he complained. He wanted to punch, rip, and burn the book. It was ruining his entire summer. "Who cares if I got a few Cs? I aced all my standardized tests, didn't I?"

"You sure did," his mom said. "That's why finishing the book should be easy."

"But I've been reading it all week." She didn't respond.

This was one of her tactics when she wanted him to settle down. Loop huffed for a few moments. Then he said, "Where's Rubén?"

His mom looked at him suspiciously. "Don't go thinking *he's* going to change my mind. We discussed this. You need to spend less time with magic and more time with books so you can appreciate your education. Besides, he's helping Grandma, so it's just you and me right now."

Loop knew he had lost this battle, so he stomped to his room. He plopped on the bed, put in earbuds, and turned on a sound track of traffic noise. He closed his eyes and imagined living in a giant city with six-lane freeways and skyscrapers, where no one cared about your grades or made you read books. He hoped the honking cars and revving engines would help him forget his frustration, but no luck. When he opened his eyes, the book was still there, waiting.

He sighed, opened it, and started to read again. That's when something interesting happened. In magic, a transformation is when you change something into something else—like turning a golf ball into a soccer ball. As Loop read, he started to experience a transformation in himself because he was changing from someone who hated the book into someone who liked it, all because he was getting the monster's point of view and, believe it or not, the monster wasn't scary. Sure, he looked hideous, but he was exactly like a kid trying to figure out the world. He wanted friends, just like Loop wanted friends. He wanted to learn how to read, just like Loop wanted to learn about magic. He wanted to go out and have fun—*just like Loop!* But no one gave the monster a chance because of how ugly he was. Every time he showed himself, people screamed and ran. They judged him, and Loop could totally relate because *he* got judged, too.

Loop decided to draw the monster, but he didn't want his version to look like everybody else's. *They* always drew a large body with a square green head and a zigzag of stitches on the face. But Loop remembered what Mr. Garza said about taking information from different places and creating something new, so he thought about the Frankenstein movies and the descriptions in the book and started sketching. He drew about a dozen versions of the monster but was unhappy with all of them. Then he had an aha moment. The monster was made from different body parts. So he gave the monster one eye that was wide and round and another that was almond shaped. Then he gave him one ear with a giant lobe, and another that was normal size but pierced. He also gave the monster one muscular, hairy arm and another flabby, hairless arm. Finally, he gave him two left hands and two right feet.

"You sure are ugly," he said to the picture, but he was pleased. It had taken several tries to get the drawing just right, and the extra time was totally worth it.

He thought about reading some more, but after two hours in his room, he was truly going stir-crazy. It was almost three o'clock. He'd been stuck at home all day. He *had* to get out of there. Then he heard Rubén's voice. Finally, the guy was home, so Loop gathered up his drawings and took them to the kitchen.

allied arts—
performance arts
closely associated
with magic

DOMINIC

ONCE AGAIN, DOMINIC'S PARENTS met at the Burger King in Refugio. They just waved at each other, both of them staying in their cars. Dominic didn't even *try* to make them talk.

"How was your trip?" his mom asked as he fastened his seat belt.

"It was great!" he answered. While she drove, he told her about the meals his stepmom cooked, the silly games Maria Elena played, and how he and his dad fished at Mustang Island, watched the Corpus Christi Hooks play baseball, and swam at Hurricane Alley, a water park with a wave pool, a lazy river, and lots of water slides. He was so excited by his own story that he hardly noticed the drive. He couldn't believe how quickly they reached the Victoria city limits sign. "And the best part," Dominic said, "is that Dad totally gave me permission for the magic competition. The whole gang from Corpus is going."

His mom smiled, but she rubbed her temple, too. "That's great," she said. "I'm sure y'all are going to have a wonderful time in Houston."

They finally got home. Even though Dominic was glad to be back, he also dreaded the chores waiting for him. He'd been gone two weeks, which meant lots of dust on the furniture, leaves on the balcony, and towels in the hamper, but when he walked into the apartment, it was surprisingly clean. In fact, it was *more* than clean—it was *organized*. He immediately noticed that his mom's self-help books on the shelf had been placed in alphabetical order according to the author's last name. Just like in a library! When he went to the pantry for a snack, all the boxes were on one shelf, the cans on another shelf, and the jars on their own shelf, too. The items were even categorized—a neat row of canned soups, a second row of canned vegetables, then canned beans, the cereal boxes grouped together and the pasta boxes grouped together, not to mention the orderly arrangement of jars. He peeked into the junk drawer where they threw random things like pencils, business cards, coupons, paper clips, coins, and glue sticks. Usually, when you needed something, you had to dig around, but not anymore. It was too *neat* to be a junk drawer. It looked like a tiny museum instead.

His poor mom! She must have been so bored while he was gone, because this was some intense cleaning.

He glanced at her. She was on the sofa, flipping through TV channels.

"Do you need me to do anything?" he asked. He couldn't believe he actually wanted a chore, but he felt guilty about leaving her alone.

"No," she said. "It's all taken care of."

"I could wash the car," he suggested.

"It's washed," she said. She put down the remote, propped her feet on the coffee table, and leaned back to watch HGTV. "It's vacuumed, too," she added. "Even the windows are clean. Didn't you notice?"

Dominic shrugged. He'd been too busy rambling about his trip to notice the car.

He didn't know what to do, so he put away his duffel bag and headed to Conjuring Cats. When he got there, it seemed as if the entire city had decided to buy magic. Ariel and Mr. Garza weren't around, and Mrs. Garza was all flustered as she tried to answer questions, point out merchandise, and ring up orders.

When she saw Dominic, she waved him in. "Thank goodness you're here. I'm all by myself today. Can you show these nice people the Allied Arts section while I work the cash register?"

"Sure thing," Dominic said.

The items sold in Allied Arts weren't for magic. They were for acts that involved juggling, fire breathing, clowns, or balloon artists. One afternoon, Dominic had tried balloon art because he thought his little sister might enjoy a long, skinny balloon twisted into a poodle, heart, or funny hat, but he gave up because the balloons kept popping. Dominic helped a man who wanted plastic bowling pins for a juggling act, and after he showed him the options, he helped a lady who asked for tarot cards. These were cards with cool pictures on them like a sad moon crying over a dog, a wolf, and a lobster; a woman petting a lion as if it were a kitten and not a ferocious beast; or a magician wearing a wizard cap and holding up a wand. Even though he liked the pictures, Dominic usually left the tarot cards alone. They were for fortune-tellers, not magicians. The lady who bought them looked like a gypsy with her giant hoop earrings, flowing skirt, and shawl. She knew the juggler, and they shared information about an upcoming fair.

As they chatted, Dominic considered how jugglers, clowns, and fortune-tellers were allies of magicians, and he wondered if they ever betrayed one another the way *his* allies, Loop and Z, had betrayed him.

It took thirty minutes for the store to clear out, and that's when Dominic asked about Ariel and Mr. Garza. "Where are they?"

"They're working," Mrs. Garza explained. "Once in a while, Señor Surprise performs at birthday parties. He makes Ariel go, even though she complains about it." She lowered her voice. "I think she's jealous because he's a lot better at magic."

Dominic smiled. He couldn't imagine Ariel being jealous of *anyone*, because she always thought *she* was the best.

"Are they coming back soon?" he asked. "I was hoping they could give me advice for my routine."

"They'll be gone awhile," she said. "But you're welcome to wait in the Vault. Maybe you can find some inspiration there."

Dominic nodded and stepped through the purple velvet curtain.

force—
occurs when a
magician gives the
spectator the illusion of
free choice

LOOP

WITHOUT BOTHERING TO SAY hello to Rubén and his mom, Loop spread the pictures on the table. "Look. Here's proof that I'm totally reading *Frankenstein*." And then he explained why the monster had mismatched body parts and how he had created a unique version because instead of copying, an artist takes bits and pieces from different places to create something new. "Just like Dr. Frankenstein created something new," he found himself saying. "Only my 'new' thing isn't ugly like his." He looked at his own pictures. "Well, maybe it *is* ugly, but I made it like that on purpose."

This made his mom and Rubén laugh.

"You have all these rough drafts and put a lot of work into this," Rubén said. "That's good."

His comment gave Loop hope. "That's why I deserve a little break now. Don't you think?"

Rubén nodded.

"So I can go to Conjuring Cats?" Loop asked, all excited.

"Sure, why not?"

He was about to head out when his mom jumped in. "Wait a minute. We've discussed this. You are not finished with the book, and—"

"Let him go," Rubén insisted. "He's been working all day."

"Yeah," Loop said. "It can't be 'all work, no play' *all* the time."

"It certainly *can*," his mother said.

Rubén took her hand and kissed it. "*Por favor, mi amor.*"

She always gave in when Rubén flirted with her. "Fine," she said. "Since you guys are ganging up on me, what choice do I have? It's two against one."

In magic, a skilled card handler will ask the spectator to choose a random card, but it's never truly random, since the card that gets picked is the one the magician wants. It's called a force. It worked for magicians, and it worked for Loop, too, because he'd forced his mom to give him the answer he was looking for—a giant yes for Conjuring Cats.

Loop cheered, and Rubén raised his fist. Loop almost gave him a fist bump, but he changed his mind at the last minute and offered a handshake instead. "Thank you," he said, all formal.

Rubén looked disappointed, but he shook Loop's hand anyway and kept an upbeat voice. "You're welcome," he said.

Loop went to his room to grab his wallet. As he was leaving the house, he heard his mom complain to Rubén. "If you keep spoiling him, he'll never respect you."

Loop shook his head. *It's not about respect*, he thought. *It's about trust.*

He didn't want to dwell on his family's Big Lie, so he focused on reviewing the magic routine he'd been planning for the convention. Fifteen minutes later, he reached Conjuring Cats, but he didn't go into the Vault right away because he wanted to buy some supplies.

"I need latex skin, a rubber knife, and some fake blood," he announced as soon as he saw Mrs. Garza.

"You know where they are," she said.

He went to the aisle where they kept costume supplies

and quickly grabbed the latex skin and fake blood, but he couldn't decide what kind of weapon to buy. He thought he wanted a knife, but then he saw axes and swords. They would totally improve the "awesome" level of his routine. He picked up a sword and then an ax and pretended to stab and hack. They didn't weigh anything because they were made of plastic. "Nah," he decided. Swords and axes were for lopping off heads, amputating arms, and slicing people in half. He had no intention of doing major bodily harm in his routine. "Just *minor* bodily harm." He chuckled to himself. Yup, he needed to stick to his original plan, so he turned his attention to the knives, settling on one called the Terror Blade. It had a picture of a man with wild hair, lunatic eyes, and a muzzle. "This is perfect!" Loop said.

As he paid for his items, he chatted with Mrs. Garza, asking about Mr. Garza's gig and complaining about staying home all week. Then he headed to the Vault, expecting it to be empty, but as soon as he pushed back the purple velvet curtain, he saw Dominic. When he remembered how Dominic had ruined his chop cup, he got *insanely* mad, just like the psycho on the Terror Blade package.

Loop's teeth were clenched, but he still managed to snarl, "You!"

ditch—
when a magician gets
rid of an object that is
no longer needed for
his routine

Z WAS HEADED TO Conjuring Cats, too, and as soon as he entered, he spotted Loop going through the purple velvet curtain. He rushed into the Vault, barely saying hello to Mrs. Garza as he ran by the counter.

"You!" he yelled as he swooshed through the curtain.

Then Dominic yelled at *him*. "You!"

For a few seconds, they all glared at one another. If they had been superheroes, their eyes would be Tasers and they'd be on the ground shaking from spasms. That's how angrily they stared. Then all of them yelled at once.

Z shouted at Loop. "You cut up my Svengali deck. Now it's useless!"

Loop shouted at Dominic. "My chop cup doesn't work anymore, so you owe me twenty-two dollars and fifty cents!"

And Dominic shouted at Z. "Because of you, my quarter shell is all messed up!"

Then they got personal. Loop called Dominic a know-it-all, Dominic called Z a crybaby, and Z called Loop a freak. Then Z brought up the time his bike got covered in bird poop because his friends put it under a tree where hundreds of grackles roosted, and Loop mentioned the time he chipped his tooth because he fell when they all raced with their shoes tied together. Dominic complained about the time they destroyed his favorite Transformers action figure by lassoing it with strings of Black Cat firecrackers and lighting them up to see if Optimus Prime was really the strongest and bravest of all the Autobots. Then they threw out nicknames they hadn't used since forever—calling Z Buster because he fell off a trampoline and busted his lip, Dominic Mr. Toot because he accidentally farted in class, and Loop Chango for no reason at all, except that he hated to be called "monkey." And when they ran out of old nicknames, they invented *new* ones right on the spot! Like Fungus Foot, Toilet Clogger, Slobber Boy, and Stink Bomb! Z didn't like arguing, but no way was he going to back down. His friends wouldn't back down, either, so this fight had definitely turned into the biggest, wildest, loudest, meanest, "everything-est" of all the fights they'd had since kindergarten.

Z seriously wanted to ditch his friends! He had absolutely no idea why Dominic kept blaming him for a messed-up quarter shell, because Z had never touched it. As far as he was concerned, his friends were lying. What he couldn't figure out was why *they* thought *he* was lying, too.

So he and his friends kept arguing, shouting that so-and-so was guilty because of this-and-that. No one would admit anything. No one would apologize.

They might have argued till midnight, but a shrill whistle startled them. Z and his friends turned toward the sound and saw Mrs. Garza at the door. "Settle down! All this noise is bad for business!"

"But—" Loop tried.

She held out her hand like a cop stopping traffic. "I don't want to hear it." She took a deep breath. Then she said, "I don't know what's going on with you boys, but whatever it is, you better make peace now or get out of this store." She shook her finger at them and then abruptly left.

Z felt bad. Mrs. Garza had been so nice to him, and if it weren't for her, he never would have auditioned to get access to the Vault. The last thing he wanted was to make her angry, but he couldn't let his friends get away with ruining his cards and accusing him of something he didn't do.

For a moment, the boys were quiet. Finally, Dominic went to a table and sat down. Z joined him, then Loop did as well.

"Look," Dominic said in a calmer voice. "It's okay if the quarter shell is messed up. I wasn't going to use it for my routine anyway."

"For the last time," Z said, all exasperated, "I didn't mess up your quarter shell! I never touched it. You just have to believe me."

"If you want Dominic to believe you," Loop said, "then you'll have to believe *me* about the Svengali deck. How could I mess it up when I didn't even have it?"

Z knew this was an outright lie. "Okay, then," he said, challenging him, "explain why it was in your locker."

Loop shrugged. "Honestly, I don't know how it got there. I don't even use that locker."

Z remembered opening Loop's locker and seeing that it was practically empty.

"Besides," Loop said, "why were you looking in my locker?"

"Because," Z answered, "Ariel told me to."

Loop thought a moment. Then he looked at Dominic. "Ariel told me you were using my chop cup for strange experiments before you went to Corpus."

"And it was Ariel," Dominic added, "who said Z was practicing with the quarter shell, which seemed really weird because"—he glanced at Z—"you only like card tricks."

They sat quietly for a while, but it didn't take them long to reach the same conclusion.

All at once, they shouted, "Ariel!"

misdirection—
turning the audience's
attention away from
secret moves

DOMINIC

IT HAD TO BE ARIEL, Dominic realized. She was the common denominator in all their stories. But why would she do this in the first place?

"I watch crime shows," Loop said. *"Law and Order, CSI,* anything with Sherlock Holmes, and if there's one thing I've learned, it's that—"

"You're innocent until proven guilty?" Z guessed.

"No, it's that—"

Dominic knew the answer. "You need to demonstrate three things in a court of law: means, motive, and opportunity."

"Let me finish!" Loop took a deep breath before continuing. "The thing I've learned is that people who don't *look* like they have a mean streak are sometimes the worst criminals—like the guy next door or the cute girl."

Dominic nodded. True, Ariel was the common denominator *and* she was a cute girl who didn't seem like she could be so mean, but he wanted to investigate before giving her the guilty verdict. "Let's work this out," he suggested. "One"—he held up a finger—"Ariel has the means to mess up our stuff because she knows all about magic. Two"—he held up a second finger—"she's definitely had the opportunity because she's here all the time. And three..." He held up a third finger, but he couldn't find a reason for his third point. "Well...um...I'm not sure about Ariel's motive."

"That's right," Z said. "Why would she ruin our stuff and then frame us? It doesn't make any sense."

The boys were stumped. Then Loop said, "I know one way to find out." He pointed to Ariel's locker, the one with the giant gold star.

As much as Dominic wanted to learn the truth, he also wanted to respect Ariel's property. "We shouldn't touch her things," he said.

"Why not?" Loop asked. "She touched *ours*."

"Yeah," Z said. He was already heading to the locker. "We wouldn't think of doing this if she hadn't messed with us first. Besides, *she* told *me* to peek in Loop's locker, so she can't really blame us if we look in hers." He opened the door and took out Ariel's notebook. "I bet we'll find lots of answers in here," he said.

He brought it to the table and was about to open it when Dominic stopped him. After all, what if Ariel had her most secret, deepest desires in there? "This is supposed to be private," he said, putting his hand on top of the notebook before Z could open it. "Like a diary."

"Even better," Loop replied. "I've been curious about this notebook all summer. Remember what I said about the cute girl being the bad guy? I bet she has sinister plans for all kinds of stuff—like formulas for crazy poisons that make your fingernails fall off or designs for a machine that can suck up the oxygen in a twenty-mile radius, making all the people, even innocent little children, gag and claw at their throats as they suffocate to death."

Dominic couldn't help chuckling at his friend's wild imagination. "But seriously," he said. "She probably has love notes in there or stories about being a princess. Isn't that what girls think about? It's what *my* sister thinks about."

"No way," Z said. "I have lots of sisters. Sure, they talk about boys sometimes, but they're more interested in who's fat and who's skinny, or who's rich and who's poor. They watch TV all the time, and it isn't Disney stuff. They like talk shows, which are really *yelling* shows with husbands and wives screaming at each other for cheating or being lazy or spending all the money. My sisters like court TV, too. And the whole time they're watching, they're talking about how dumb people are. That poem about girls being sugar and spice and everything nice is a bunch of baloney."

"You said it," Loop agreed. "Girls are mean."

Dominic shrugged. "I don't know," he said, thinking about his mom, his little sister, and Mrs. Garza. "*Some* girls are nice *and* smart."

Z brushed aside Dominic's hand and started to open the notebook. "Trust me," he said, "this isn't private because Ariel told me she's writing her memoir, which is a book about your life."

Dominic rolled his eyes. The last thing he needed was for *Z* to give *him* definitions. "I know what a memoir is."

"So do I," Loop said. "You guys would be surprised by all the stuff I know."

"So think about it," Z continued. "People write memoirs

because they want *other* people to read them. We're actually doing Ariel a favor by taking a peek."

Dominic thought a moment. Maybe Z had a point. If Ariel intended for no one to see her notebook, then why would she keep it in a locker without locking it up? Besides, how else could they discover the truth?

"Well," he said, "when you put it that way."

He and Loop gathered around as Z flipped to the first page. It had a bunch of doodles. In fact, Ariel doodled a lot. She loved lists, too. One was called "Stupid Love Stories" and she wrote, "*Romeo and Juliet* because they both die. *Titanic* because Leonardo DiCaprio sinks into the freezing ocean and dies. *Ghost* because ghosts can't hold your hand or kiss you or even call you on the phone because they're incorporeal, which basically means dead. And another stupid love story? *The Fault in Our Stars*—do I even have to explain?" Another list was called "Useless Talents" with things like singing the alphabet backward, reciting poetry in Klingon, and "getting the title of a random *SpongeBob SquarePants* episode, like 'Squidville,' and then offering a scene-by-scene summary. Seriously, I know a guy who does this, and to make matters worse, he's proud." Dominic actually thought this was a very useful talent, since it meant the guy had a great memory, great enough to store every *SpongeBob SquarePants* episode ever made.

Ariel also had outlines for magic routines and pages filled with magic-related brainstorms. Those pages were quite interesting, but lots of stuff was boring, especially when she wrote about her daily activities. Dominic was glad to learn that every morning began with Ariel brushing her teeth, but did she have to record it all the time?

He was ready to declare Ariel innocent, but then they found the following entry:

MY DAD

- AKA Joe Garza; CEO of Conjuring Cats, specializing in retail services for magicians, illusionists, escape artists, psychics, clowns, and hobbyists.
- Former president of the TAOM and a member of the Order of Willard.
- Award-winning performer who is best known by a sombrero instead of a top hat and by the stage name Señor Surprise.
- Upstanding citizen with a college degree, an excellent credit score, and no cavities or enemies.
- A victim of devious manipulations by three strangers!

POSSIBLE CAUSES OF MY FATHER'S RECENT GULLIBILITY

- My father is experiencing a midlife crisis whereby his unfulfilled dreams have left him disappointed, delusional, and depressed.
- My father has become extremely sensitive and vulnerable after I tried to make my own flash paper using a paint solvent and crystals from inside a road flare. Apparently, tree houses are poor substitutes for science labs. I accidentally caused a fire, burning down the tree house and then the tree, and even though my father was glad that I narrowly escaped death, he was devastated to learn that certain books and props from his "secret" collection did not escape.
- My father is the victim of body snatching, and his likeness is now possessed by an alien.
- Whatever the cause, he is not the same after the arrival of these three devious *strangers*.

Dominic couldn't believe it. How could Ariel blame them for her father's behavior? Besides, as far as he was concerned, Mr. Garza was a nice guy. So even if he *had* changed, he'd changed into something good.

"So that's why she kept ignoring us," Loop said. "She thinks we're devious."

Z nodded and then said, "Maybe, but why would she mess up our stuff? We need to keep reading."

Dominic agreed, and the boys flipped through a few more pages. Ariel had pics of Diamonds and Spades with thought bubbles that said things like, "That's TUNA-licious," "Purrhaps," and "¿*Cómo se dice 'meow' en Español?*" She also liked to copy her name over and over again—Ariel, Miranda Ariel, Ariel Garza, Miranda Garza, Miranda Ariel Garza, M.A.G., and Miranda G. She used different fonts, too, and different colored pencils. Sometimes, she turned the letters into pictures, like adding a chimney to the "A" or a top hat to the "L."

Finally, the boys found an entry with more clues:

SUBJECTS OF OBSERVATION: 3
AMATEUR MAGICIANS (AKA NOOBS)

- Always competing.
- Evidence of deep jealousies.
- Confusion over ownership of property.
- Lacking in communication skills.

- Susceptible to suggestion, which has made possible the successful execution of my plan.

"There it is!" Dominic exclaimed. "Proof!"

"Proof of what?" Ariel asked as she entered the Vault. Then she spotted the boys with her notebook.

torn and restored—
when a magician cuts up
something like paper or
string and then makes it
whole again

LOOP

LOOP *KNEW* THAT ARIEL was the human version of a computer virus, planting glitches in the perfectly good program of his friendship with Dominic and Z. *Always the cute girl*, he repeated to himself. He shaped his hand into a gun, pointed at her, and pretended to shoot. "Pow! You are so busted."

Ariel marched straight to the table and grabbed her notebook. "This is private!"

"No, it isn't," Z said. "You told me you were writing your memoir."

She was stumped, but only for a moment. "This is the *rough draft*. You aren't supposed to read the rough draft. You're supposed to wait till it's on the bestseller list. And then you're supposed to *buy* a copy and stand in a really long line for my autograph—*if* you can get to New York or Los Angeles, because no way am I doing a book signing *here*. I need a city with millions of people. By the time my memoir is finished, I'll be famous, and I probably won't even remember you guys. *This*"—she waved her notebook—"is nothing close to the final story. I haven't even picked my pen name. You are *not* supposed to read someone's memoir until after she has figured out her pen name!" As an afterthought, she added, "And a logo. Every artist needs a logo."

"Blah, blah, blah!" Loop said. "All this talk about being famous is just another form of misdirection. Quit trying to avoid the *real* topic."

"That's right," Dominic said, "and the real topic is *not* your memoir."

She crossed her arms, hugging her notebook against her chest. "What is it, then?"

"Are you serious?" Loop was flabbergasted. "You lied and framed us! You told me Dominic did weird experiments on my chop cup, and you told Z that I took the Svengali deck."

"And then you planted evidence in Loop's locker," Z said, "forcing me to get mad at him."

"I didn't force you guys to do anything," Ariel replied. "And trust me, I didn't have to work very hard to get you mad at one another. I know all about your rivalries."

"We don't have any rivalries," Dominic said.

"And all your jealousies," Ariel went on.

"We're not jealous," Loop said.

"And every single insecurity that runs through your minuscule minds."

"We're not insecure," Z said, and then, "Are we?"

Ariel laughed. "Of course you are—and jealous *and* always competing against one another. Each of you wants to be the best and hates it when the other guy wins, no matter how serious or silly the competition." She walked to her dad's desk, opened a drawer, and dumped the notebook inside. "How about *this* for some honesty? If you guys were better friends, you wouldn't have been so eager to believe my ... little stories."

"Those were *not* little stories," Loop said. "They were lies!" He didn't mean to shout, but he was so sick and tired of people lying to him.

No one spoke for a whole minute. Then Dominic said, "We thought you were our friend."

"We thought..." Z hesitated. "We thought you were nice."

"She never had *me* fooled," Loop said, crossing his arms.

If they had shouted at her, Ariel would have shouted right back, but scolding her in this quiet way must have made her feel ashamed. For the first time *ever*, she didn't have a comeback. She looked down at her shoes and her ears got red. Then she clenched her lips as if holding back tears, but only for a second. Loop could tell she didn't want to cry in front of them, no matter how bad she felt. She'd run out of the room first.

Before they could say anything else, Mr. Garza walked in. He was carrying his sombrero and a backpack. Today he wore a black T-shirt with the Conjuring Cats logo. "Is everything okay in here?" he asked without really noticing that Ariel looked like someone who had just been suspended from school. "Mrs. Garza says you were shouting earlier."

Loop glanced at Dominic, since he was the one who usually spoke to the authority figures when they were in trouble. "We were," Dominic admitted, "but everything's okay now."

Mr. Garza opened his backpack. Instead of books, it

held his magic props. "So what were you fighting about?" he wanted to know as he put the items away. "It's bad for friends to be angry."

"It was just a misunderstanding," Dominic said. "But we're okay now. Honest."

That's when Mr. Garza noticed Ariel. Instead of suspended, she now looked like someone who had just been expelled. He squinted at her suspiciously. "Did *you* have anything to do with this?"

She looked up, her eyes wide. Loop almost snitched. After all, Ariel wasn't the only one who liked to cause trouble. But his friends jumped in first.

"Ariel wasn't even here," Z said.

"That's right," Dominic added. "We were actually fighting about stuff that happened a long time ago—like, before we even met you guys."

Loop nodded. There was enough truth in Dominic's statement. Some of the stuff they brought up *had* happened years ago, even though that hadn't been the main reason for today's fight.

"Sometimes we argue a lot," Dominic explained. "We didn't mean to bring it into the Vault."

"We won't do it again," Z said. "We promise."

"*Bueno*." Mr. Garza seemed satisfied. "We're all amigos here, right?"

The boys nodded, and Ariel sighed with relief. Then Mr. Garza hung his sombrero on the wall, grabbed another mean dog T-shirt, and stepped into the restroom to change.

When he closed the door, Ariel said, "Thanks for not telling on me. I would have been grounded for sure."

"Whatever," Loop said as he grabbed his bag of merchandise. "We're out of here." Dominic and Z grabbed their things, too, and they all left the Vault.

As they walked down the street, Z said, "Did you see the look on her face? I thought she was going to cry. I started to feel sorry for her."

"She wasn't going to cry," Loop said. "But if she had, I wouldn't have felt sorry for her. Not one bit. Especially now that she owes me twenty-two dollars and fifty cents for my chop cup."

"She owes me, too," Dominic added.

"And me!" Z said. "I got really mad!" He looked at Loop. "I was ready to punch your face in."

Loop shrugged. "It would have been pointless because I would have blocked it and knocked you out with an uppercut."

"Well, if somebody tried to punch me," Dominic said, "I would have responded with a body slam, lucha libre style."

"That stuff's fake," Z said.

"Yeah," Loop said, "if you want to end a fight, try a rear naked choke like an MMA fighter."

"Or an arm bar," Z suggested.

"I don't need a rear naked choke or an arm bar if I'm fighting *you* guys," Dominic teased. "You'd probably tap out if I pulled your pinkie finger."

They all laughed. Then Loop held up his little finger and in a silly voice said, "Leave my pinkie alone!"

And Z pretended to be a sportscaster. "The referee calls an end to this contest at one and a half seconds in the very first round for a win by pinkie-pull submission." He lifted Dominic's hand. "Let's hear it for Dominic the Cominic!"

Dominic blew kisses at an imaginary crowd.

Z then turned his attention to Loop. "Let's take a closer look at that pinkie," he said. "How badly is it injured?"

Loop held up his finger. "I'm just glad I have *two* pinkies, because I really need them to pick my nose."

The boys cracked up. They couldn't stop themselves. They got tears in their eyes, and their stomachs started hurting from all the laughter. It felt so good to be friends again.

Soon they found themselves at the intersection with the stoplight, so Loop pushed the button for the cross sign. As they waited, he remembered the last time they had been there. They were fighting and ran across the street at different times, all that traffic between them, and he smiled because now they were going to cross together.

Miser's Dream—
a miser is a person who tries to
keep all his riches to himself;
in magic, this refers to a
trick where coins appear
out of nowhere

FOR THE NEXT THREE weeks, Z spent all his time looking for jobs and practicing magic. He hadn't worked at the apartment complex since Dominic had returned because he knew Dominic got an allowance for doing chores at home. As for Dominic's neighbors, they were supposed to call Z if they needed extra help, but so far, no one had touched base.

Z actually missed going to the complex. As promised, Dominic's mom had introduced him to her friends, and they had paid Z to do things like walk dogs, put plants in bigger pots, or scoop out leaves from the pool when the regular pool guy got sick. Z had done jobs for Dominic's mom, too, and while he worked, they talked. She had some great stories. She used to run track in high school, and during out-of-town track meets, she would sneak out with friends in the middle of the night to hang out at twenty-four-hour places like Whataburger or Walgreens, whatever was close by. "It's a wonder we never got in trouble," she'd said.

But ever since Dominic got back, Z was stuck bugging his own family and neighbors. Once in a while, they gave him something to do, but it wasn't enough. He desperately needed more work.

At least he had time to work on his Ambitious Card routine. So far it looked good, but he needed a twist in order to stand out, especially if others were doing card tricks, too. So he went to Conjuring Cats to see if Mr. Garza had any suggestions.

When he stepped into the store, Ariel was at the counter flipping through magazines.

"Where's your mom?" he asked, since Mrs. Garza was usually the person who worked up front.

"There weren't any customers, so she decided to take a lunch break. She's in the Vault."

Z glanced at the purple velvet curtain, wondering if he should disturb Mr. and Mrs. Garza.

"It's okay to go back there," Ariel said, somehow reading his mind. Z nodded, but before he could head toward the Vault, Ariel stopped him. "Hey, Z?"

"Yeah?" he said.

"So...um...well...are you getting ready for the competition?"

"Yeah."

"Do you know what trick you're going to do?"

"Yeah."

"Why don't you show it to me?" She closed her magazine and cleared space on the counter.

"I don't think so," Z said.

"Why not?"

"You'll probably make fun of me."

"I won't. Promise." She crossed her heart to prove it.

Z tried to believe her, but he couldn't. He just didn't trust her anymore. "That's okay. Maybe another time," he said, and he left her there, alone.

When he stepped into the Vault, Mr. and Mrs. Garza had just finished lunch. Today Mr. Garza's T-shirt had a picture of an angry pit bull with the words MEAN MUGGIN' written across the top. Z told the Garzas about his routine while they rinsed their plates and wiped the counters. "I would love to see what you're working on," Mrs. Garza said, but then she had to leave because the bell from the shop jingled and Ariel peeked in to tell her someone had entered the store.

Luckily, Mr. Garza was still in the Vault, so he took a seat at the table. "Show me what you've got."

Z grabbed the deck of cards from his back pocket, shuffled them a few times, and began. He went through the whole routine without messing up. He was so proud of himself, especially when Mr. Garza clapped and said, "Bravo! Your card-handling skills have improved immensely."

"Thanks," Z said as he did a few cuts. "But...I don't know...it's not good enough. I need something more if I'm going to win—like an interesting twist. Do you have any ideas?"

Mr. Garza stroked his chin for a while. "I think I do," he said.

They spent the next hour revising the routine. Mr. Garza's idea for an interesting twist required some rope, a slight modification to the cards, and lots of practice. Once Mr. Garza demonstrated the moves, he returned to his computer so Z could rehearse.

Z did the sleights over and over. Most were familiar, but a couple of them were new. With so much repetition, his hands began to move automatically, leaving him time to think about the Ambitious Card routine and how one card insisted on rising to the top no matter how many times you stuck it in the middle of the deck. Of all the card tricks, this one made the most sense to Z because, like the card, he wanted to be at the top—to be *first*! That's why he needed to win this contest—to show everyone that he could be the best at something.

He visualized the contest, especially the moment when they announced the winner—him! And he saw himself taking a bow and accepting the trophy, the whole audience giving him a standing ovation. Wouldn't that be great? A standing ovation just for him!

He caught himself smiling about it, and then all at once his daydream shut down. He froze, the cards locked in his hands.

Mr. Garza must have noticed that Z had stopped practicing, because he turned around and asked, "*¿Qué pasó?* Is the trick too hard?"

"No," Z said. He took a seat, put down the cards, and pushed them away. He felt so defeated.

Mr. Garza left his desk and took a chair across the table. "Talk to me."

Z sighed. "I don't know why I'm practicing because I can't even go to the convention. I have all these brothers and sisters, and after buying groceries and paying bills, my parents are broke. We never go on vacation. We never go *anywhere*. And all I ever get is hand-me-downs. I know we're not as poor as other people. We always have food. And we have cable and Internet, and I know you don't absolutely need those things, but what about other stuff? Like this convention? I tried to get the money myself, but it's impossible. I'm just a kid. Even with a head start from my parents, there's no way I'm going to make enough!"

Mr. Garza thought for a moment, and then he said, "I have just the thing for you." He went to the wall, took down his sombrero, and put it on. Then he went to the cabinets and grabbed a big coffee can, handing it to Z. "Look inside."

Z looked. "It's empty."

"Good, good." Mr. Garza took the can back. "Look here," he said, "nothing up my sleeve, right?"

"You're wearing a T-shirt," Z said.

"That's right. That's how you know there's nothing up my sleeve." He placed the can on the table, straightened

284

his sombrero, and shook out his hands. "Now watch what Señor Surprise has for you," he said, all dramatic.

He picked up the can and, once again, showed Z that it was empty. Then Señor Surprise peeked into it, too, his face exaggeratedly disappointed. He shook the can a little, nothing. He shook it again, still nothing. He shook it a third time, and it jingled. Señor Surprise peeked again. Now his face showed total amazement. He reached into the can, pulled out a quarter, and made a big show of waving it in front of Z's face. Then Señor Surprise held the quarter to the sky, rubbed his fingers together, and one coin turned into two. He dropped them into the can. Now it made even more noise when he shook it. But he wasn't finished. He sneezed and out came a quarter. He tugged his earlobe and out came a quarter. He scratched his underarm—another quarter!—each of them clinking in the coffee can. Then he bowed, and when he bent forward, several coins rained from his sombrero and dropped into the can, clinking and jingling as Señor Surprise shook it like a kid with a piggy bank.

"That was great!" Z said.

"It's called the Miser's Dream." Señor Surprise took off his sombrero. He was Mr. Garza again. "If you want to see a great Miser's Dream performance, look for Jeff McBride's version." He looked at the ceiling, all dreamy. "I can only aspire." Then he shook the can again. The quarters were still inside. Somehow Z thought they would disappear once the trick was over. "Cup your hands," Mr. Garza said. Z did as he was told, and Mr. Garza poured the coins into his hands. "You can keep them."

Z counted. Twelve quarters. He was grateful for every cent he could get, but twelve quarters were not going to solve his problem.

"I don't get it," Z said. "How is this trick supposed to help me? I mean, we both know three bucks isn't enough, and *I* know you can't make coins appear from thin air."

"Maybe not," Mr. Garza said, "but sometimes things that seem empty"—he pointed at the coffee can again—"are actually full of hidden treasures."

Z still didn't understand, but he was too embarrassed to ask for a better explanation. His best guess was that Mr. Garza was trying to make him believe in magic, *real* magic, but Z knew the world didn't work that way. In the *real* world, money didn't fall from the sky, from your nose, or from the brim of your hat. Z could blow on his fist and wave a magic wand all he wanted, but when he opened his hand, it would still be empty.

Homing Card—
in magic, this trick
features a card that
continually returns to
your hand after you
put it away

LOOP

WHILE Z SPENT THREE weeks trying to raise money, Loop spent them reading *Frankenstein*. It had taken him such a long time to get through the book—partly because he spent time with his chores, magic, and friends, but also because he didn't like the last chapters, when the monster started killing people. Usually, Loop didn't mind blood and guts—like in movies and video games. But when the monster got violent, Loop felt betrayed. He'd put the creature in the "good guy" category like the cartoon monsters in *Beauty and the Beast* and *Shrek*. Wasn't the moral of the story supposed to be "Don't judge a book by its cover"? But *this* book seemed to be saying the opposite—sometimes ugly on the outside meant ugly on the inside, too.

In Loop's last set of pictures, the monster was a shadow figure in the dark corners of rooms and gardens. The book ended with him hiking through the Arctic, so Loop drew a snowy landscape with giant footprints disappearing into the horizon.

When he was all done, he took the pictures to his mom. She was at the kitchen table with the newspaper, but she put it aside when Loop joined her.

"Here," he said, placing them in front of her. "I read the entire book, so no more summer homework, okay? I need to focus on my magic. The contest is less than two weeks away."

"Okay," she said. "That's fine." She carefully examined the drawings. "So tell me. Did you like the book?"

Loop shrugged. "I guess," he admitted. "But with those old-fashioned words, it was hard to understand sometimes."

"Most people wait till high school to read it."

"Really?" He straightened up, feeling proud in spite of himself. "That's cool. I guess I'm not as dumb as you thought."

His mom smiled at him. "I never thought you were dumb. Just lazy. There's a big difference. Look at what you can do when you work hard." She nodded at his drawings. "I just want you to apply yourself."

Loop thought a moment. "Okay," he said, grabbing his work. "So can I apply myself to magic now?"

She rolled her eyes, but she chuckled, too. Then she waved him away. "Go, go. Practice your magic."

Loop called his friends to invite them to Conjuring Cats. Z said he'd stop by after his job search, but Dominic said he'd meet him right away. They timed it perfectly, arriving at the same moment.

When the boys entered the store, they saw Mr. Garza wearing a T-shirt with a picture of dogs smoking cigars and playing poker. Dominic said, "How come you always wear dog shirts when your shop is called Conjuring *Cats*?"

Mr. Garza grumbled, so Mrs. Garza answered for him. "He wanted to call the shop Houdini Dogs or Top Hat Dogs, but I wanted Conjuring Cats."

"I got outvoted," Mr. Garza said, glancing at his wife and daughter. Ariel was reorganizing the DVD shelf.

Mrs. Garza said, "Sorry, hon. Conjuring Cats has alliteration, and everyone knows that alliteration sells. That's why you're called Señor Surprise. Remember?"

Mr. Garza just grumbled again.

He held a ladder steady while Mrs. Garza climbed up to hang some posters. Meanwhile, Diamonds had her claw stuck in a curtain, and Spades had knocked over an arrangement of cups and balls. Then Diamonds got free, and she and Spades chased each other all over the store, running between Mr. Garza's legs and knocking over more stuff.

"Ariel!" Mr. Garza called. "Come and get these cats out of here!" Then, to the boys, he said, "Should have gotten dogs."

Ariel rushed over to shoo Spades away. Then she picked up Diamonds. The cat closed its eyes and purred.

"Want to pet her?" Ariel asked Loop.

"Nah," he said.

She wouldn't take no for an answer. "Here." She offered the cat. When he backed away, she turned to Dominic.

"Maybe another time," he said.

The boys didn't say anything else. They just headed to the Vault, leaving Ariel behind.

Once they were alone, Dominic said, "She's been trying to talk to me all month."

"Me too," Loop replied. "But I don't trust her for a minute."

"Maybe she feels bad. Maybe she's sorry."

"Has she apologized?" Loop asked.

Dominic shook his head.

"Has she replaced your quarter shell?"

Dominic shook his head again.

"That's right. And I'm still without a chop cup, and don't forget about Z's Svengali deck." Loop took a quarter from his pocket and walked it across his fingers. "She wants us to drop our guard so she can fool us again."

"How can you be so sure?" Dominic asked.

"Because that's what Rubén's doing," Loop explained. "Ever since I found out he's not my dad, he's been supernice because he wants me to forget he lied."

Dominic said, "But it's not like Rubén *changed* when you learned the truth. He's *always* been nice."

"Yeah, but only because he feels guilty," Loop answered.

"I don't think so," Dominic said. "My dad's nice to me, buys me stuff, too, and not out of guilt."

"Are you kidding? He is *so* guilty! Didn't he divorce your mom, move to Corpus, and start another family?"

Dominic thought a moment. "Okay, you've got a good point, but I don't hold it against him. I guess I'm used to it."

Loop walked the quarter through his fingers again, then did a French drop, and repeated the whole process. "Well," he said, "I'm not used to the idea of Rubén not being my true dad. This whole time he was just *pretending*."

Mr. Garza stepped into the room at the moment Loop finished his sentence. "Who's pretending?" he asked.

"My fake dad," Loop answered.

Mr. Garza raised an eyebrow, curious. So Loop told him the story of how he thought Rubén was his father and how the whole family, even his cousins, knew the truth—that Loop's real dad was some loser. And how Rubén was now trying to buy Loop's love by taking his side all the time and giving him a big allowance. But no way was Loop falling for *that* trick. "My real father might be a loser, but at least he's not a fake like Rubén," Loop said.

Mr. Garza seemed to study Loop's problem. "Hmm...," he mumbled as he stared into the distance for a while. Then he said, "Do you know what a black sheep is?"

Loop answered sarcastically because this was such a dumb question. "You mean, a sheep that is black instead of white?"

"He means a *symbolic* black sheep," Dominic said. "Like how you have a family, but there's always one person who doesn't fit in. You know, everybody likes pizza but one person eats liver instead?"

"Whatever," Loop said, unconvinced. "I don't see what

sheep—no matter what color they are—have to do with my family."

"Sit down, and I'll show you." Mr. Garza pointed to the table, so the boys sat down. Then he grabbed his sombrero and a deck of cards, and joined them. "Look," he said, holding out his arms. "Nothing up my sleeve, right?"

"You're wearing a T-shirt," Loop pointed out.

"That's how you know I'm not hiding anything."

He took off his Meathead baseball cap and left it on the table, upside down, so the cap looked like a bowl. Then Mr. Garza put on the sombrero so he could be Señor Surprise again. He took four cards and dropped the rest into the baseball cap. "This is about a red family," he said, turning over the first three cards. They were all hearts. "And a black sheep," he added, turning over the fourth card, the ace of spades.

"Now, once upon a time, the red family told the black sheep, 'You don't belong.'" He dropped the ace into the cap. "But the black sheep wouldn't stay away." He pointed at the cards in his hand. Now there were three—two red and the ace of spades.

"They pushed him away again." Señor Surprise dropped the ace of spades in the cap and showed them the two remaining cards. Both were red. "But the black sheep wouldn't stay away." He pointed at his hand. Now he held *one* red card and the ace of spades.

"The red family got really mad because they did not want that black sheep around." He dropped the ace of spades in the cap and revealed the red card left in his hand. "But?" He let the question hang in the air as he slowly turned the card. When he showed the face again, it was no longer red—it was the ace of spades!

"The black sheep," Señor Surprise whispered, "would not stay away."

Loop and Dominic clapped.

"How'd you do that?" Dominic asked. "Did you use false counts? Double lifts? Were you palming that card the whole time?"

"If you really want to know, then study the Homing Card," Señor Surprise said as he squared the deck. "Now back to work for me and back to work for you."

He took off the sombrero but left it on the table. Then he put on his baseball cap and returned to his desk.

Loop had no idea why Mr. Garza had shown him that magic trick. As far as he could tell, it had nothing to do with his family. He flashed back to a time he had to draw a family tree in school. For an example, his teacher drew a flow chart and used dotted lines to add relatives who had married into the family or been adopted. Then she asked the students to draw their own flow charts. Dominic followed the instructions exactly, using dotted lines for his stepmom and sister and thick lines for his parents, while Z taped two pages together to make room for all his brothers and sisters. Loop did the assignment, too, but he drew an actual tree, a winter tree with sharp, pointy branches like knives in the sky. His mom was the trunk, and Rubén was a kite stuck in the branches. When his teacher asked him to explain, he said that sometimes families grabbed random people just like trees grabbed random kites.

What he *didn't* say was that he was waiting for a big gust of wind to blow that kite away.

Oil and Water—
a trick in which cards
are mixed up and then
magically separated into
groups of black cards and
red cards

DOMINIC THOUGHT MR. GARZA'S Homing Card made total sense, but he could tell that Loop was still confused. "It's a metaphor," he said. "I can explain it if you want."

"No," Loop said. "I get it."

Dominic didn't believe him, but he let it go because he'd made a secret promise to stop giving answers all the time. He didn't want to be called a know-it-all ever again.

To change the subject, he said, "So what are you doing for the magic competition?"

Loop cheered up immediately. Then he showed Dominic his Terror Blade as he described the routine, his voice getting louder at each step of his trick. "First..." he began, "and then...and then...and then...and finally a giant freak-o-rama!" Loop threw out his hands and made exploding sounds. Dominic's eyes widened. His friend's trick certainly had shock value. "I'm not even going to talk," Loop went on. "It's all about the visuals. If Ariel could win without patter, then so can I." He took his rubber knife and pretended to stab his guts. Dominic desperately wanted to say that Japanese samurai once stabbed their guts to commit suicide in a ritual called hara-kiri, but then he remembered—*Stop acting like a walking* Wikipedia!

Just then, Loop's phone rang, and after a few minutes of "But I just got here" and "You promised to let me work on my magic," he said, "Okay, but you owe me."

"You have to go home?" Dominic guessed as his friend pocketed the phone.

Loop nodded. "My grandma's waiting for me. She probably brought a new candle and wants me to pray."

"Maybe you can pray for good luck at the convention," Dominic suggested.

"I'm not supposed to be selfish."

"Then maybe you can pray for *me* to have good luck."

Loop laughed. "You got it. One good-luck prayer coming up." He and Dominic fist-bumped, and Loop was off.

So Dominic found himself alone. He spent the next thirty minutes thinking about his routine. He was going to perform a mentalism trick with a book as the central prop. It was called *Lost: Fifty True Survival Stories.* It wasn't a trick book like the magic coloring book that instantly added color to its drawings and then made them disappear. No, his book was normal. You could get it from any Barnes & Noble, and with a small modification, turn it into something magic. He had already mastered the moves, but he was struggling with his patter. He could write all kinds of research reports, no problem, but *this* was hard. Thankfully, Z showed up, so Dominic decided to ask him for help.

"Really?" Z said. "You want *me* to help *you*?"

"Yeah. What's so weird about that?"

"I *never* help you," Z said. "*I'm* the one who's always confused, and *you're* the one who always explains things."

"Well, this is different. I've got writer's block. I've had it all summer. But every time *you* do a trick, you know exactly what to say."

Z straightened up and pointed at himself. "That's because I'm an artist."

"And I'm a bookworm," Dominic said as he held up his book of survival stories.

Z rubbed his hands together. "Okay, so what are you going to do for the competition?"

"I'm going to read someone's mind."

Z closed his eyes a minute, and when he opened them, he had a blank face.

"I know what you're doing," Dominic said. "You're trying to block my telepathy."

"Oh, man! You're really good. That's *exactly* what I was thinking!"

"Ha-ha," Dominic said, deadpan. Then, "So you want to see my trick?"

"Of course!"

Dominic hesitated. He hadn't shown his trick to anyone, including Mr. Garza, even though *he* was the one who'd taught it to him. "You want to see it, too?" he asked.

Mr. Garza didn't turn from the computer or pause typing when he answered. "I'll watch it later. I've got some Internet orders to process."

"Quit stalling," Z said to Dominic, "and show it already."

"Okay, okay," Dominic replied, but he was feeling nervous. What was wrong with him? If he couldn't show his trick to one of his best friends, then how was he going to show it to a room full of people? How was he going to show it to the judges?

He took a deep breath to calm his nerves. Then he showed Z the book, a pencil, and a notepad, and he went through the motions of the routine. His technique was flawless, but there was one problem—a *major* problem. Z didn't laugh at the jokes, and he seemed bored—even after the big revelation at the end!

Dominic snapped his fingers as if to wake up his friend. "Are you still trying to block my telepathy? Because I totally proved that I could read your mind."

"I know. And it was really cool." Z smiled, but it was the same smile Dominic got from his dad when he performed the Die-ception trick. He had bombed then, and he had totally bombed now.

"You didn't like my trick," Dominic concluded. "I can tell."

"Yes, I did. It was..." Z struggled for the word. "Interesting."

"Really?"

Z chuckled. "Yeah. As interesting as watching a green banana turn yellow."

"That's cold," Dominic said, but he was laughing in spite of himself.

"Nah," Z said. "I'm just picking on you. If you lived in my house, you'd hear stuff like that all the time. Like last week, I was Zero-G and yesterday, I was the zoo-maniac. That's my brothers' new thing—calling me z-words. They'll probably call me a 'zylophone' next."

"But 'xylophone' starts with—" Dominic stopped himself. "Okay, back to the subject," he said. "Give me your honest opinion about my trick."

Z paused. "I liked it, okay? It's just... well..."

"Tell me!" Dominic insisted. "Don't hold back. I need the truth."

"Well... like I was saying... it was good, but you kinda lost me. The patter went over my head, and my mind started wandering. But it's probably just me. My mind is *always* wandering."

Dominic slumped in his chair. "No, it's not you," he said. "My trick is boring, and *I'm* boring. I'm too much like my mom."

"What does *that* mean?" Z asked.

"She's all-work-no-play, and so am I."

"But that's a *good* thing, isn't it?"

"Yes," Dominic answered. "It's a good thing when you're in school, but not when you're trying to win a magic competition. Why can't I be like my dad? He's always the life of the party. But my mom? She never has any fun."

"Are you kidding?" Z said. "Your mom's a lot of fun. She's one of the most interesting people I know. She was a star athlete in high school, and then, before you were born, she and her friends used to go primitive camping. They would hike to the middle of nowhere and live off the land— no electricity or phones or toilet. Just nature. That's insane! And your mom did it. She was so adventurous. She has all kinds of stories about her primitive camping days."

Dominic shook his head. Was he imagining things? How did Z know so much about his mom?

"You're making this up," Dominic said.

Z crossed his heart. "Am not."

"How can you possibly know all this?"

"Because," Z said, "I hung out at your place when you were in Corpus."

Dominic put the pieces together, and then he had an aha moment. "Are *you* the one who organized my house?"

"Yup. Your mom paid me, and she introduced me to all your neighbors. She knows I need money for the convention. If you ask me, she's the nicest lady on the planet. She always has snacks for me, too. I *never* get snacks at my house. So you see? Your mom's not boring at all."

"I guess," Dominic said. "But..." He needed a few seconds to process what he wanted to say. "Okay, so let's say that my mom's cool and my dad's cool, but the way they ignore each other is totally *uncool*. They act like they have nothing in common, but how can that be true when they used to be married? And even if it *is* true, they still have me. Just once—like maybe on my birthday or something—I'd like to hang out with both my parents at the same time."

Z had nothing to say. He just held up his hands and shrugged.

Then Mr. Garza interrupted. "Let me show you something."

The boys turned to him. Mr. Garza wasn't processing orders anymore. He was actually facing them. He'd been listening to the whole conversation. If eavesdropping were an Olympic sport, he'd have a gold medal for sure.

He headed to the table, donned his sombrero, and showed them his arms. "Nothing up my sleeve, right?"

"That's exactly what you said a little while ago," Dominic pointed out. "Besides, you're still wearing the same T-shirt."

"Ah, yes. I do this on purpose, and that's how you know. No sleeves, no secrets."

He shuffled a deck of cards. Then he took three black cards and three red ones. "This is oil," he said, showing the black cards one by one, then placing them facedown to his right. "And this is water," he said, showing the red cards and placing them facedown to his left. "Let's see what happens when you try to mix oil and water." He made a new pile, alternating cards from the black and red piles. "Just give it a few seconds," he said as he snapped his fngers. "And you'll see that the oil rises to the top." When he turned the cards around, the black cards were on the top and the red cards were on the bottom. They were no longer alternating.

"Maybe you don't believe me, so let's do it again—this time with the cards facing up." He made a new pile, alternating red and black. Then he turned over the cards and squared the deck. "Give it a few seconds," he repeated with a snap, "and the oil rises to the top." He turned the cards. They weren't mixed anymore.

Now Señor Surprise took the remaining deck and started shuffling. "It doesn't matter how much oil and water you have, or how much you stir the two ingredients." He shuffled, cut the deck, and shuffled once more. "The oil will always rise to the top." This time he did two ribbon spreads, and when he flipped them over, the top row was black while the bottom was red. "And that's because," he concluded, "oil and water do not mix."

Z shook his head in disbelief. "I *must* learn that trick," he said. "That was awesome!"

"No," Señor Surprise said. "If you want to see an awesome rendition of the Oil and Water card trick, then watch Rene Lavand. He performs it with one hand and"—he added a dramatic tone—"*No lo puedo hacer más lento.*" Then he translated in a whisper, "I can't do it any slower."

He let the boys think about this for a while before removing the sombrero and returning to his desk.

"That's it?" Z asked. "Aren't you going to explain what it means?"

"Dominic knows," Mr. Garza answered.

Dominic nodded. It was true. He knew *exactly* what Mr. Garza's trick meant, and he knew exactly what he needed to do about his family.

Coins Across—
a trick where coins
magically travel from
one hand to the other

Z AND DOMINIC SPENT the rest of the afternoon writing clever patter for the mentalism trick, but every time Dominic said the words, he sounded like someone reading the ingredients on a Froot Loops box.

Z could only shake his head. "You sound like a robot. Put some *feeling* into it."

"I'll try," Dominic said. "But doing the routine while saying the words is hard. It's like trying to sync two separate parts of my brain."

Z nodded even though he had no idea what his friend was talking about.

After a few more rehearsals, the boys decided to leave. On their way out, Ariel asked if they were coming by tomorrow. They said maybe, even though they planned to come every day till the convention.

And the convention was all they talked about during their walk home. It was only ten days away! Dominic had printed out the program, so he showed Z the lectures being offered and the list of magicians who were going to be in the stage show. These guys could levitate, perform telekinesis, and make tigers disappear.

"I can't wait!" Dominic said, all excited.

Z felt excited, too, but when Dominic turned in to his apartment complex and left Z alone, reality hit. Z did not have enough money, and even if he worked 24-7, he wouldn't earn enough to register for the convention *and* the competition. At this point, he didn't care if he won or lost. He just wanted to compete. Even if he came in last, he'd still be ahead of the person who didn't try, but right now, *he* was that person. "Last again!" he shouted to the sky.

As soon as he reached his house and stepped inside, his brothers looked up from their video game. "Hey, zillionaire," they teased. So that was the new z-word. If only it were true.

As usual, the house was full of people. Z's father and brother-in-law inspected a ceiling fan that rattled too much. Copycat set the table, and Smiley chopped veggies for a salad. Meanwhile, his oldest sister and his mom made french fries and catfish. He spotted Bossy in the kitchen, too, but she wasn't cooking or mixing or chopping anything. Instead, she was shouting orders that everyone ignored. Z's cousin stood in a corner and practiced the trombone. He was going to be in the high school marching band, and since he'd be playing at football games, he practiced as loudly as he could. His trombone was louder than the sound effects from Z's brothers' Need for Speed video games, louder than the crackling grease in the kitchen, louder than the dog barking for scraps, and louder than the five or six conversations happening at once. All this noise was giving Z a headache, so he went to his room.

Z knew he was supposed to love his brothers and sisters, but part of him wished he was an illusionist who could make them disappear so he could have the house and everything in it—the food, the space, but mostly his parents' (and the dog's) attention—all to himself.

He shut the door to his room, plopped on the bed, and stared at the ceiling. Then he took his cards from his pocket and mindlessly practiced a sleight called "the pass." It let him secretly move a card to the top or bottom of the deck. Z practiced passes the way some people popped their knuckles or doodled. One pass, two passes, three. It calmed him down. He loved the feel of the cards, the slight breeze as he riffled them, the sweeping sound they made as they slid against one another.

Z studied the cards, did one more pass, and then rolled over and stuck them under his pillow. This whole summer was just a silly dream, and he was stupid to think that he'd have a chance to compete at the convention.

After a while, he heard his mom calling. Dinner was ready. He headed to the main room, expecting a long line for food. But when he got there, everyone was already sitting down, even his mom! Then he noticed other weird things, too.

- Weird thing #1: When the whole family gathered—like on July Fourth—there wasn't enough room, so he had to sit at the "baby table" with Boxer Boy and Copycat because they were the youngest. And it was a lousy fold-up table with fold-up chairs that gave you a numb butt if you sat in them too long. This time, however, Smiley was sitting in the uncomfortable chair.

- Weird thing #2: When the whole family gathered—like on Thanksgiving—his dad sat at the head of the table and Z's brother-in-law sat at the *other* head of the table. This time, however, his brother-in-law sat off to the side. That meant that his normal seat was available, and since it was a place of honor, it couldn't possibly be for Z—yet it was.

- Weird thing #3: When the whole family gathered—like for the Super Bowl—everybody stood in line for food, oldest to youngest, which meant Z got the skinniest cut of meat and the hardest crust of bread. But this time, a giant plate of food waited for him. And not only did the plate have a lot of food, but it also had the most golden french fries, the thickest fish fillet, and the moistest square of corn bread. Everyone knew his mother always burned the edges, but this slice came from the *middle* of the pan.

Z expected a prank to reveal itself, but nothing happened. His whole family just smiled at him. So he got all self-conscious. He double-checked his zipper in case his fly was open, and then he wiped his nose in case he had boogers. But everything was fine, so what was his crazy family up to?

"What are y'all looking at?" he asked.

"You are so cute," Smiley said. "I have a friend who said that if you were a puppy, she'd totally adopt you."

"Woof, woof," Z said with no enthusiasm, but everyone laughed as if he'd told the funniest joke. "Okay, this is weird. What's going on?"

"*Sientate*," his father said, still giggling.

Z went to the head of the table, and when he pushed back the chair, he saw an envelope on the cushion. His family always dumped mail on the table, so he expected an electric bill or an advertisement, but this envelope had "For Ezio (the zillionaire)" written on it.

"What's this?" he said, picking it up. It was thick. Maybe the prank was in the envelope. Maybe his brothers had stuffed one of those springs in there, the kind shaped like snakes. They sold them at Conjuring Cats. Like a jack-in-the-box, the coiled snake jumped out when you opened the container.

"Hurry! Open it," Bossy said.

Z carefully opened the envelope, tilting it away in case a snake jumped out. But when he broke the seal, nothing happened. He peeked inside, shaking his head because he couldn't believe what he saw. There were twenties, tens, and lots of fives and ones. The envelope was full of money! He started to count. With the money he'd saved on his own, he had almost $500, and since his friends had already offered to share a room, the money was enough for the convention!

He looked at his family. They still had goofy smiles on their faces.

His dad said, "It's a gift from all of us. Everybody pitched in."

"Even me," his cousin said.

"Your brothers and sisters came up with the idea," his mom explained.

"Yeah," Copycat said. "We came up with the idea after we saw how hard you were working. You haven't played at all this summer. Work, work, work. That's all you do."

"But where did you get the money?" Z looked at Boxer Boy, Copycat, and his cousin because they didn't have jobs.

"We collected cans," Boxer Boy said. "Every day, we rode our bikes around the neighborhood and picked up cans. Then we took them to the recycling plant, and they paid us."

"This town is full of litterbugs," Copycat said. "So we made lots of money."

"The rest of us saved money from our jobs," Toenail said.

"We got something else for you," Z's oldest sister added. She reached under the table and pulled out a large bag from JCPenney. Because she was at the other end of the table, nearly everyone touched it as they passed it along to Z, so it truly felt like a gift from all of them. Z couldn't wait to peek inside, and when he did, he discovered black slacks, a black dress shirt, a red tie, and a new leather belt.

"No more hand-me-downs," his mother said. "If you're going to compete, you need to look like a professional."

Z's heart raced with excitement. This extra money meant he could go to the convention. He could do the Ambitious Card in front of a real audience. Ten minutes ago, he was broke, but now he was rich! He thought about a popular magic trick called Coins Across, how quarters magically traveled from one hand to the other. That's exactly what was happening here, with money moving from his family's hands to his. Then he remembered the day Señor Surprise showed him the Miser's Dream. It made total sense now. Sometimes the empty can was actually full. Sometimes money *did* appear out of nowhere!

"I don't know what to say," Z admitted.

"Try 'thank you,'" Bossy suggested.

But Z didn't say thanks. Instead, he showed his gratitude by going around to hug everyone. It took a long time, since there were so many people. When he had finished, he took his seat at the head of the table and began eating from the heaping plate of food. That's when he realized that for once, he was first—and he was first where it really mattered: his home.

impromptu act—
when a magician
performs on the spot
with whatever items
are nearby

DOMINIC

DOMINIC STEPPED INTO HIS apartment, quickly said hello (his mom was reading a book called *The Power of Positive Thinking*), and rushed to his room, making sure to close the door. He needed to make a plan—not for the magic competition, but for his parents. They were oil and water, like Mr. Garza explained, and because oil and water didn't mix, Dominic could never get them to talk. It was driving him nuts! He wanted to spend time with his entire family, so he *had* to get his parents to cooperate—even if it was only for one day.

Dominic turned on his computer and looked for articles and statistics about kids with divorced parents. Maybe he could make a chart with the benefits of . . .

He stopped himself. *When will I stop acting like a text-book?* he wondered. *Showing my parents a chart with a bunch of numbers and articles is the worst idea in the world!*

Nope. He had to figure out another way to persuade his parents to talk. Maybe . . . he tapped his desk . . . maybe he could make them feel sorry for him.

He went to the mirror and pouted, scrunched up his fore-head, and drooped his eyes, but he couldn't make himself look like those sad puppies on the adopt-a-pet commercials. He'd have to cry. How hard could it be? After all, Maria Elena could make herself cry in less than a minute. So Dominic tried forcing out tears, but nothing happened. It didn't make sense. Hadn't he read that half the body was made of water? So where were the tears? Why didn't they gush out when you most needed them?

Maybe he had to think of sad things—like in every super-hero movie when the good guy's best friend gets shot, or learning that the video game console he just bought after months of saving his allowance was useless because of a newer, better model. These were very sad things, but Dom-inic still had no tears.

He thought about chopping onions or eating a dozen jalapeños, but that required a trip to the kitchen. His mom would see him for sure and realize that he was fake-crying. So he went to the restroom and rubbed soap in his eyes. They burned a little and a few tears leaked out, but mostly, he just blinked a lot. Who knew crying was harder than chewing gum while rapidly reciting tongue twisters like "If two witches were watching two watches, which witch would watch which watch?"

Dominic threw up his hands. *I'm overthinking this. I just have to jump in like a magician performing an impromptu act.*

He returned to his room and Skyped his dad, and when his dad answered, Dominic said, "I've got something very important to say, so promise me you won't hang up, no matter what."

"Did something happen? Is everything okay?"

"Just promise me," Dominic pleaded.

"Sure, I promise."

"Good. Now hold on a minute. I'll be right back."

Dominic rushed out before his dad could reply. He went straight to his mom and said, "I have to show you something in my room. It's very important, so promise me you'll take a look."

She put down her book and started to stand. "What happened? Did you break something?"

"No, I didn't break anything. Do you promise to stay in my room when you see what I have to show you?"

"Yes," she answered. "I promise."

She followed him, but when she got to the doorway and saw Dominic's dad on the computer, she stepped back.

"What are you up to?" she said.

And his dad said, "That's what I'd like to know."

Dominic grabbed his mom's arm and pulled her straight to the chair by his desk. She sat down, but she swiveled away from the computer screen. She wouldn't look at his dad, and his dad wouldn't look at her. Instead, they both stared at Dominic.

"Here's the thing," Dominic began. "No matter what I do, you can't stand being in the same room at the same time. Even now, you're avoiding each other." His mom sighed, and his dad looked down. "When you drop me off at Burger King in Refugio, you can't even sit with me to eat french fries. When I have a program at school, you take turns going, instead of going together. And if it's you picking me up at the house, Dad, you text to let me know you're in the parking lot because you don't want to knock on the door and risk seeing Mom, which is ridiculous because every time Mom thinks you're coming over, she disappears." He glanced at his mom. "You know it's true, Mom. And I can never tell both of you a story. When something exciting happens, I have to tell *one* of you. Then I have to repeat the entire story again, and it's never as good or as interesting as the first time I tell it. And I know that you and me are a family, Mom." Dominic turned to his dad. "And I know that you and everyone in Corpus are my family, but my families are never *together*. So I feel all divided. I just wish...I wish..." He was getting a little choked up. Who knew that talking about his feelings would bring out the tears. "I wish you weren't oil and water!"

"Oil and water?" his parents repeated, though not in exact unison.

"Yes, because oil and water just. Don't. Mix!" His parents stared at him, stunned. This was the first time Dominic had ever raised his voice. "Don't look at *me*," he said. "Look at each other. Say something!"

After a few seconds, his dad took a deep breath and then spoke to his mom. "So...how are things going?"

Dominic's mom hesitated, but then she answered. "Okay, I guess."

There was a long, awkward pause.

"Been anywhere interesting lately?" his dad asked.

"Like where?" his mom replied.

"I don't know. Like a concert or a movie. Have you gone to any interesting vacation spots?"

"And when am I supposed to go on vacation?" Dominic's mom crossed her arms.

"When Dominic's in Corpus. Didn't you go on any trips when you had some time to yourself?"

She narrowed her eyes. "Do you *really* think I had time to myself? Think about it. When am I supposed to go on vacation? I have to work!"

His dad shook his head. "Why do you always take things so seriously?" he asked.

"Why do *you* always take things so lightly?" she replied.

And then they started discussing who worked harder and who was more responsible and who wasted time and who never relaxed, and all of a sudden, their discussion turned into an argument, so Dominic stomped out, slamming the door behind him. He was so mad! He almost didn't care if they talked to each other, especially if it meant they were going to fight.

He went to the bathroom and splashed water on his face. Then he stared at his reflection. His eyes were red, this time not because of soap. As he looked at himself, he noticed other things, too. He got the shape of his eyes from his dad, and the shape of his nose from his mom. He got his hair color from his dad, and his skin color from his mom. Maybe oil and water didn't mix when you were doing card tricks, but they had definitely mixed in him, and since both of his parents loved him, that meant they had to love each other, too. Why couldn't they see that? They were the adults. They were supposed to be smarter than him.

He needed a glass of water, so he headed to the kitchen. On the way, he stopped at his bedroom door. His mom was still in there, but since the door was closed, he couldn't hear anything. He didn't know if his parents were talking or if they had hung up already. He decided to leave them alone, but the suspense was killing him. He drank water. He put away some dishes. He went to the front door and peeked out the peephole, then to the balcony to look at the trees. He paced and nervously popped his knuckles. Twenty minutes had passed! He *had* to know what was going on, so he barged into his room.

As soon as he stepped in, he saw his stepmom and Maria Elena on the computer screen. "Dominic!" his little sister called.

"We're getting to know each other," his mom explained.

"Meanwhile," his stepmom said, "your dad's making arrangements so we can all watch you at the magic competition."

"Really?" Dominic said. *"Everybody?"*

"Yup!" Maria Elena clapped her hands. "And we're getting matching T-shirts and making posters and coming up with cheers!"

"Well, I don't know about all that," his stepmom said. "Why don't we wear Dominic's favorite color to show our support?"

"Is his favorite color purple?"

Dominic said, "No, I like black or red."

Maria Elena frowned, but after a moment, she decided that she could wear a red T-shirt if it would help Dominic win. A few minutes later, his dad returned, and everyone had to reposition themselves so the camera could catch all their faces.

"Did you hear the good news?" his dad asked.

"Yeah. Everyone's going to Houston to see me perform."

"How about the special handshake," his dad said, and even though they couldn't touch through the computer, they went through all the motions. Then, his dad got serious. "We're sorry, son. Your mom and I had no idea you were mad at us. You deserve to feel like you have a whole family."

"So we're putting aside our differences," his mom said.

"No more oil and water?" Dominic asked, and his parents nodded.

"What's oil and water?" Maria Elena asked. "Are we going to cook something?"

Everybody laughed, and then Dominic described Mr. Garza's magic trick. Maria Elena said it sounded interesting, but she still thought they should invent a special recipe.

They spent a while longer discussing plans for the convention, and then they logged off Skype. That's when Dominic's mom sighed. She seemed sad all of a sudden.

"What's wrong?" he asked. "Aren't you glad you're going to Houston?"

"Of course. It's just…" She paused a moment. "Talking to your father makes me uncomfortable," she admitted. "We have a past, and it didn't work out. So part of me feels like I failed. Then when you're with *him*, you have so much fun, and even though I know that fathers and sons have a special bond, I get kind of jealous. I worry that you're lonely over here, especially when I leave you alone while

I'm at work. When I think about how nice it is for you to have a house full of people in Corpus, I get all panicky."

"Why?"

"Because . . . because what if you decide to live with *them* instead?"

Dominic had never thought about the situation from his mother's point of view. No wonder she got a headache whenever he mentioned his dad. No wonder she worked so hard to make sure he had everything he needed. All this time, she was scared of losing him.

"I'm sorry if I made you feel that way," he said, giving her a hug. "This is my home. I'm not lonely. I have you and my friends."

She gave him a real hard squeeze before letting go. "You have no idea how good that makes me feel. And you're right. You have very nice friends. Z is especially helpful."

Dominic laughed. "He's totally hoping you'll adopt him."

She laughed, too, and then she stood up. "Come on. Let's go," she said.

"Go where?"

"Bowling."

"Do you even *know* how to bowl?"

"As a matter of fact, young man, I was a proud member

of the Gutters and Pins bowling team when I was in middle school."

"Bet you hit more gutters than pins," Dominic teased.

"Trash talk, huh?" She thought a moment. "First person to make a strike gets a week's vacation from chores."

Dominic held out his hand so she could shake it. "You're on!" he said.

prestidigitation—
another word for
skillful sleights
of hand

LOOP

LOOP PACKED HIS SUITCASE, checking and double-checking the props he needed for his magic trick, and then he kneeled at the *retablo* with the little statue of La Virgen de Guadalupe. He usually only did this when his grandma was around, so it felt weird praying by himself. But since he was headed to the convention, he needed all the help he could get. First, he said the Our Father and Hail Mary. Then he gave thanks for a few things. And then, he started his petitions. "Okay, O.G.," he said. "It's almost show-time. I really want to win, but that's not what I'm asking for because Grandma says I shouldn't be selfish. So I'm making a petition for myself *and* for my friends. The last time we did magic in front of people, we all messed up. But we've been practicing all summer. That has to count for something, right? So please help us do our tricks without messing up." He paused, and then he said, "Amen."

Just then, someone knocked on his door. Loop stood up. "Come in," he said. It was Rubén.

"Almost ready?" he asked. "Your friends will be here in a minute."

Dominic's mom was driving them to Houston today, Thursday, so they could help Mr. Garza set up his booth in the dealers' room. They were going to spend Friday attending different convention events, and on Saturday, they'd compete.

"Yeah," Loop said. "I have everything I need."

"*Almost* everything," Rubén said. He held out a baseball cap. It was white with a giant black "W" for the Warriors baseball team. "It's my lucky hat. I wore it when we won district."

Loop took it and traced the "W" with his finger. His whole life, that hat had taken an entire shelf of a curio cabinet in the living room. Rubén *never* wore it. The only time he touched it was to wipe off the dust.

"I want you to have it. Maybe it'll bring you good luck, too."

"Thanks," Loop said. He knew he should say something else, but before he could find the right words, the doorbell rang, and a few seconds later, his friends rushed into the room.

"Come on," Z said, all impatient.

Dominic grabbed Loop's suitcase and started heading out. "My mom wants to reach Houston before rush hour."

Loop looked at his friends, who were already in the hallway, and then he looked at Rubén.

"Go on," Rubén said. "Have fun. Your mom and I will get there tomorrow, okay? Grandma's coming, too."

Loop put on the cap, and instead of a handshake, he offered his fist. Rubén smiled as they did a fist bump with explosion sounds. That had always been *their* version of a special handshake.

Houston was two hours away, but it felt like a fifteen-minute drive because the boys talked the whole time. Soon, they were in the big city. Dominic programmed the GPS, and his mom asked them to be quiet so she could hear directions to the hotel.

As they drove through Houston, Loop thought about all the cityscapes he drew and how he was looking at a real-life version of his pictures. They were on a ten-lane freeway—five lanes in each direction! It made the widest streets in Victoria look like sidewalks. At certain points, three or four Houston freeways met in a tangled mess of roads that turned and overlapped one another like a heap of spaghetti. Then there were miles of shopping centers, apartments, hospitals, and office buildings. Loop loved the idea of living in a place with so many choices and people. *I'm definitely moving here someday*, he decided. When they got to the downtown area, he was even more amazed. He loved the skyscrapers, especially those with mirrored windows. He pretended that each had a landing pad for spaceships and that he was really traveling in a hover car.

They finally reached the hotel. It was so fancy, with chandeliers and a grand piano in the lobby. While Dominic's mom went to the front desk to check in, the boys wondered which of the guests were magicians. Every time they saw another teen, they elbowed each other and whispered, "Think he's in the competition, too?"

"Here are the keys," Dominic's mom said. The boys were going to share a room; Dominic's mom would stay next door in case they needed anything.

Loop glanced at the room number. "We're on the twenty-sixth floor!" He couldn't contain his excitement. The tallest building in Victoria was twelve stories, so this was more than twice as high! As soon as they got to the room, the boys rushed to the window. The city looked like a giant 3-D map. From that high up, the people were tiny ants and the cars were Hot Wheels toys.

After they settled down, Loop called Mr. Garza's cell phone, but Ariel was the one who answered. "Where are you guys?" she asked.

He gave her the room number, and a few minutes later, she knocked. She wore an official-looking badge around her neck. Dominic and Z seemed glad to see her, but in Loop's opinion, Ariel still owed him for ruining his chop cup. He wasn't as mad as before, but he wasn't over it, either.

"So first," Ariel said, "we're going to pick up your badges. That way, you have access to the convention." As they followed her to the convention area on the second and third floors, Ariel gave them an overview of how things worked. "You need to wear your badge at all times. You can take lots of notes but no pictures during the lectures, and never open any door that has an 'in session' sign." Usually she sounded bossy, but today, she sounded nice, like a tour guide.

They reached the registration area and picked up their badges. Then they went to the dealers' room, a giant area with rows of booths. Mr. and Mrs. Garza were hard at work. They gave the boys two dollies and told them to unload the van, so Loop and his friends spent the next hour walking back and forth from the dealers' room to the parking garage. He lost count of how many boxes they unloaded. Then they helped organize the booth. Mr. Garza had a few props, but mostly he planned to sell DVDs, books, and lecture notes.

"Why aren't you selling more magic supplies?" Dominic asked.

Mr. Garza waved his arm across the room. "Too much competition."

That's when Loop finally paid attention to all the vendors. There were more than twenty, and each had a different focus. One booth sold crystal balls and wizard figurines. Another sold juggling supplies, and another sold things a magician wears, like top hats, capes, and gloves. There was a booth with nothing but back issues of popular magazines like *Genii* and *The Linking Ring*, while others featured gaff cards or magic wallets.

Now that they had finished with *their* booth, Mr. Garza

stood back and examined it. He nodded approvingly. Then he reached into a bag and pulled out three Conjuring Cats T-shirts and handed them to the boys.

"Remember our agreement," he said. "I helped with your routines, so now you have to wear a Conjuring Cats T-shirt. Wear them tomorrow and make sure you walk all over the place. We need to advertise. *¿Entiendes?*"

The boys nodded. Mr. Garza sat down to rest his feet, and they stood around wondering what to do next, but before they could ask, a kid walked straight up to them. He was tall and athletic-looking, not because he had muscles but because he wore silver rec specs that were slightly tinted. Loop guessed the boy was fourteen or fifteen years old.

"Hello, Ariel," the boy said.

"Hello, Stewart." She made a hissing sound when she pronounced the "S" in his name. They had a mini stare-down, and then Ariel said, "What are *you* doing here? The dealers' room isn't open to the public till tomorrow."

"I have my ways," Stewart said. Then he looked at Loop and his friends. "So you have an entourage now?"

Ariel tossed her head like a diva. "Jealous?" she asked.

"Hardly," he replied.

"Just one of the perks of being the reigning champion

of the TAOM teen stage contest." She looked at the boys. "Stewart was the runner-up."

"Well, I'm sure to win *this* year," he said.

"Only because, as the reigning champion, *I'm* ineligible to compete."

"I'd win even if you *were* competing. You can't hide behind petals and petticoats in a close-up act. It's a lot more sleight-intensive."

"For your information," Ariel said, "my card handling is top grade." To prove her point, she took out a deck of cards and performed a cascade.

"All flourish, no substance," Stewart said, taking out his own deck and doing a perfect Faro shuffle.

"Child's play," Ariel answered, performing her own shuffle while saying, "Engblom anti-Faro shuffle." Then she performed another sleight and said, "False cut."

Stewart was quick to reply. "*Dead* cut," he said as he did the move.

"Side steal," Ariel challenged.

"Tamariz perpendicular steal," Stewart countered.

"Classic pass." She did the move.

"S. W. Erdnase pass." *He* did the move.

"Fan spread."

"Fan spread with palmed card to pocket."

"*Ribbon* spread."

"*Ricky Smith* ribbon spread with card control to top."

As they continued their card-sleight showdown, the boys' eyes pivoted back and forth like spectators at a tennis match. Ariel and Stewart did passes, palms, color changes, and culls, all in rapid succession and all perfect as far as Loop could tell.

Finally, Ariel dealt a few cards and triumphantly shouted, "Bottom deal!"

Stewart paused and smiled smugly. "*Center* deal!" But before he could perform the sleight, Ariel gasped, and Mr. Garza stood up.

"You can do that?" he asked. "The center deal?"

Stewart shrugged. "Maybe I can. Maybe I can't. You'll just have to find out when I perform."

With that, he walked off.

"What's a center deal?" Dominic asked.

"It's the one sleight I have yet to master," Mr. Garza said.

Loop couldn't believe it. He thought Mr. Garza could do every sleight that had ever been invented.

"No one gets the last word when it comes to magic. No one but me," Ariel said, her eyes like laser beams as she watched Stewart walk away. Then she turned to the boys. "Let's huddle," she said, and they made a circle just like a football team discussing plays. "Tomorrow, meet me at zero nine hundred hours by the pool. Bring your props. We must *not* let Stewart win." She put her hand in the middle of the circle and the boys did the same. "Conjuring Cats on three," she said. Then she counted off, and they cheered.

For the first time since they had discovered her diary, Loop forgot to be mad at her. Maybe she was on their side after all.

flash—
occurs when a magician
makes a mistake or
accidentally reveals a
hidden prop

DOMINIC

THE NEXT MORNING, DOMINIC and his friends met Ariel by the pool. She was sitting at a table with an umbrella for shade. As soon as she saw them, she said, "Show me what you've got."

Loop went first. He didn't have any patter. Instead, he used audio effects. Since they were on his cell phone, the sound track seemed like it came from another room. "It'll be on the speakers tomorrow," he said.

"Are the contest directors bringing speakers?" Ariel asked. "Do they have your music file?"

Loop was confused. "The contest directors?"

"Yes, you have to coordinate with them," she explained. "You can't expect them to bring a sound system without a request. Didn't you read the contest procedures?"

Loop scratched his head.

"He doesn't like to read," Z tattled.

"Are you kidding?" Loop said. "I spent the entire summer reading. I'm one hundred percent sure I read more than you, probably more than Dominic, too."

Dominic doubted it, but he didn't say anything. This was no time to argue about who read more books.

"After we finish here," Ariel said, "we'll look for the contest directors to make sure there'll be a sound system in place. If we're lucky, someone else is using a sound track, too. If not, then we'll have to brainstorm another approach."

Loop touched his baseball cap. He'd told Dominic that Rubén had given it to him. "I'm feeling lucky," Loop said.

"Good, because you're going to need all the luck you can get," Ariel replied. Then she turned to Z. "What about you?"

Z did his trick. Dominic felt very impressed by how well his friend handled cards.

"You've come a long way since the Pen-through-Dollar trick you performed at the beginning of the summer," Ariel

said. Dominic couldn't believe she was actually complimenting someone. "And," she went on, "you seem very
comfortable with your patter."

Z smiled. "Thanks!"

"But"—Ariel held up a finger—"you're not giving me
any eye contact."

"Eye contact?"

"Yes. You kept your eyes glued to the props, even when
inviting the audience to participate. Your magic is fine,"
she explained, "but your performance could use some
improvement." She included Dominic and Loop as she
continued. "The judges are looking for skill, originality,
and performance. In other words, how well can you enter-
tain the crowd? You have to look at the audience, and you
have to pretend that you're not nervous, no matter how
much you're freaking out inside."

Dominic felt his stomach twist up again. Calming his
nerves was the toughest part of magic.

"The judges will be sitting in the first or second row,"
Ariel went on, "and they'll have mean-looking faces. For
some reason, judges always have mean-looking faces.
I think they do it on purpose. It's an intimidation tactic.
Your job is to make them smile. If you make them smile,

you'll win some points." She focused on Z again. "So I suggest you give them direct eye contact. Let them know you're there to have fun and that you're not afraid of them."

Dominic couldn't help it. He moaned.

"What's wrong?" Ariel asked him. "Why do you sound like a dog taking its last breath?"

"I have stage fright," he answered. "I don't think I can look directly at the judges. I'll freeze up. I just know it."

She thought a moment. "Have you ever heard of imagining people in their underwear when you're about to give a speech?"

"Yeah," he said. "It's supposed to make them less threatening, right? You think I should imagine them in their underwear?"

"No!" she said. "Don't do that. It'll totally gross you out. Trust me. You don't want to think about people in their underwear."

"Then, what am I supposed to do?" he asked.

"Don't worry," she said. "I'm going to teach you some breathing and visualization techniques."

They spent the next hour practicing how to use eye contact and how to calm their nerves. Ariel also had tips for being more expressive and for covering your angles so you didn't flash. "Flashing is an automatic deduction," she warned. She knew those contest rules inside and out. No wonder she was the reigning champion.

"Well," she concluded, "that's all I got. The rest is up to you." She paused, closed her eyes, and took a deep breath. It was the same calm-your-nerves technique she'd taught Dominic. When she opened her eyes again, she said, "I'm sorry, guys. I caused a lot of trouble this summer, ruining your stuff and getting you mad at one another. I've got no excuse, but I'm hoping to make it up to you by helping with your routines. Will you accept my apology?"

Dominic and his friends didn't speak right away. Admitting you were wrong was tough, especially for someone like Ariel. She probably spent the last few weeks feeling terrible about what happened. She probably felt left out every time the boys went to the magic shop. Dominic was ready to forgive her, but he wasn't sure about his friends. Then Loop said, "Don't worry about it." And Z said, "We're not mad anymore." So Dominic said, "It's all forgotten." And it truly was.

Ariel sighed with relief and smiled. Then she said, "Come on, Loop. Let's go find those contest directors to see if they've got a sound system for you."

They took off, so Dominic and Z decided to attend a lecture about comedy magic. Later, Loop joined them for a lecture about stage shows. But the boys spent most of the day in the dealers' room. As it turned out, visiting the booths was the highlight of the convention. Like Mr. Garza, most of the vendors were professional magicians. They knew that the best way to make a sale was to demonstrate their props. Dominic saw tons of magic just by walking around. And every now and then, he spotted famous magicians like Bill Malone, Joshua Jay, and Jeff McBride!

Soon it was dinnertime. Loop was eating with his grandma and parents, and since Z's family hadn't arrived yet, he decided to join the Garzas. Meanwhile, Dominic's Corpus Christi family had checked into the hotel and called a restaurant to make reservations for everyone, including his mom. Dominic wondered what it would be like for everyone to sit at a table together, but sure enough, his parents sat as far apart as they could. They didn't talk much, but they didn't completely ignore each other, either. Maria Elena had a dozen questions for Dominic's mom, while his dad had a dozen questions about the convention. So most of the time, there were two conversations going on, with his stepmom switching back and forth between the topics. Every now and then, Dominic's parents talked to each other directly. He could tell they felt uncomfortable, but he was glad they tried their best to have fun.

Later, when they returned to the hotel, Dominic and his mom had a moment alone in the elevator.

"Were you nervous at dinner?" he asked.

"Yes," she said. "But after a while, it wasn't so bad."

He felt inspired. If his mom could overcome her nerves after years of avoiding his dad, then Dominic could certainly overcome his stage fright.

outjog—
to position a card so
that it stands out from
the others

EARLY THE NEXT MORNING, someone tapped on the hotel door. Z rubbed the sleep from his eyes and made his way to the peephole. His entire family waited on the other side.

"Dominic, Loop, wake up! My family's here."

"What time is it?" Loop mumbled.

Instead of answering, Z opened the door, and everyone filed in. They turned on the lights, opened the curtains, and found places to sit. Since there weren't enough chairs, they sat on the beds, not caring that Dominic and Loop were still under the covers.

353

"We brought breakfast," Z's mom said as his brothers lugged in two Styrofoam ice chests. The smell of chorizo and *papas* filled the room.

"Do I smell *taquitos*?" Loop said, finally waking up.

Dominic threw off his blanket. "Are those homemade tortillas?"

Z's brothers opened the ice chests, and it was a free-for-all with the *taquitos*—everyone talking at once and bumping into one another as they passed around napkins and drinks. The room was so crowded with Z's entire family, including his brother-in-law, cousin, *and* two friends, but he felt right at home.

After they finished eating, his dad stood up. "*Vámonos*," he said to the family. "The boys need to get ready."

"Wait a minute," Z said. He reached into the official TAOM Convention tote bag and pulled out an envelope. "You need these passes in order to see the competition." He handed them out, glad that the competitors were given free passes for family members. Unfortunately, the evening event cost five dollars per person, but since his family planned to leave that afternoon, it didn't really matter—unless, of course, Z won. But maybe it wasn't such a bad-luck thing for his family to miss the awards ceremony because if Z *did* win, he'd get to celebrate twice—once with his friends and a second time with his family.

His brothers and sisters took the passes, cleaned up, and started heading out.

"You better do good," Bossy said.

Boxer Boy punched Z's shoulder. "Break a leg, *hermano*."

Smiley just gave him a hug and smiled.

After they cleared out, the room got quiet again. Z glanced at his friends. "Well," he said, "this is it. The day we've been waiting for."

"Showtime!" Loop cheered.

Dominic had a thoughtful look on his face. "I know that we all want to win, but since that can't happen…well… can we just agree that if *one* of us wins, it's really a victory for *all* of us?"

"One for all and all for one?" Z said.

"Yeah," Dominic answered. "Like—"

"Don't say it," Loop warned.

But Dominic ignored him. "Like the three musketeers!"

Loop threw a pillow at him. "I told you not to say it!" Then Z threw a pillow at Loop, and in no time, they were all throwing pillows at one another until they realized they had to stop or they'd run out of time.

So they got ready and made their way to the contest room. Z wore his brand-new outfit, Dominic wore his everyday clothes, and Loop wore tattered jeans, an Affliction shirt, and the Warriors baseball cap.

When they got downstairs, they signed in, and the contest director reviewed the procedure and gave them the schedule. The competition started at 10 a.m. Z's name was first on the list. He couldn't believe it. For once, he didn't want to be first. Dominic's name was somewhere in the middle, and Loop's was second to last. Z saw the names of other kids, too, including Stewart's. In all, thirteen people had signed up. Seven would perform, and then there'd be a fifteen-minute break before the last six. In the afternoon, the judges would discuss their notes, and during the evening stage show, Ariel, as last year's champion, would announce the winner in a giant auditorium, right in front of all the famous magicians who'd been invited to the convention.

"Do you have any questions?" the contest director asked. Z and his friends shook their heads. "Okay, then," she said. "Good luck."

They thanked her and stepped into the contest room. Z had imagined a theater with velvet curtains and a spotlight, but this was a normal-looking room with beige carpet and walls, rows of chairs, a wide aisle in the middle, and no platform, just a clearing at the front and a table covered with a black cloth.

The boys headed to the seats reserved for the competitors, and as they walked up the aisle, Z spotted his family. They took up two whole rows! Dominic's family was there, too—everyone in a red shirt—and Loop's parents and grandma sat next to them. Then he saw the Garzas, who'd closed their booth for a few hours so they could watch the contest.

The boys sat down, and Z took a moment to size up the competition. Most of the kids looked a year or two older, like Stewart.

Then, it was 10 a.m., time to begin. The doors closed, and once everyone took a seat, the emcee addressed the crowd. "If you like this sort of thing, then this is the sort of thing you like," he joked. Then he thanked a few people, and at the end of his speech, he said, "One of the worst things about doing nothing is that you never know when you're done." Nobody laughed, but he didn't seem to care. He just glanced at the schedule and introduced the first competitor—Z.

Z stepped to the front, but before saying a word, he took Ariel's advice and established eye contact with the crowd.

"Some people have pet rocks, but I have a pet rope." He reached in his pocket and pulled out a white rope. "And here's my first pet project." He made a loop and secured it with a square knot. "I'm cutting my rope so that one becomes two." He took a pair of scissors from his pocket, snipped the top of the loop, and held it so the audience could see that he had two pieces of rope tied together. "The only problem?" he said as he wrapped the rope around his hand. "My rope is not a teacher's pet. It refuses to be two ropes tied together. Instead, it wants to be *one* rope." He unwrapped it, and sure enough, he had a single rope again. The knot had disappeared.

"Now," he said, putting the rope back in his pocket and in the same move taking out a deck of cards, "let me try a new pet project with my deck of cards." He fanned them faceup to show that it was a normal deck. Then he shuffled them, but the four of hearts popped out. He did another fan, this one facedown, but one card was outjogged—the four of hearts again. "Hmm..." he said. "All the cards are teacher's pets except for this one." He held up the four of hearts. "Let me place him in the middle and see if he stays put." He put the card in the middle of the deck, blew on it, and then he lifted the top card. Amazingly, it was the four of hearts!

"Bad card!" he said to it. "Now stay in the middle of the deck!" He pushed the card in very slowly. This time his cheeks puffed as he blew. Then he turned over the top card, pausing for a more dramatic effect and for a chance to look at the audience. Once again, the top card was the four of hearts! Z glanced at the audience, and then he spotted the judges. Ariel had called it—they had mean-looking faces—but he didn't let that distract him. "Perhaps," Z said, "I can get the rope *and* the cards to be teacher's pets if they work together." He took out the rope, pulling it taut to show how strong it was. "*Perhaps* I can make it impossible for the four of hearts to rise to the top by wrapping this rope around the deck, and tying a very tight knot." He performed those actions as he spoke. Then he held the deck out to a spectator in the front row. "Pull on the ends to make sure it's good and tight." She pulled. "Is it tight?" Z asked.

"Yes," she said.

He smiled. Then he took the four of hearts, showed it to the audience one more time, and very slowly slipped it into the middle of the deck. When it was halfway in, he revealed it to the audience, and they could see that it was definitely in the middle. After he squared the deck, he said, "This rope is wrapped tight. There is absolutely no way the four of hearts can misbehave." He held the deck out to the spectator again. "Will you do the honors and pull out the top card?"

She did, and guess what! "It's the four of hearts!" she announced, holding it so everyone could see.

Z shook his head, pretending to be disappointed. "My rope and cards refuse to be teacher's pets, and that's why my pet projects are now my *pet peeves*."

Maybe it was a lame joke, but a lot of people laughed.

Z took a bow, and when he straightened up, the crowd went wild—or rather, his *family* went wild. He could hear their whistles and *gritos*. Z should have been embarrassed, but he wasn't. He felt proud, and it didn't matter what place he got because, as he looked at his family and his friends, he realized that he'd already won.

stooge—
a person deliberately
placed in the audience
to help a magician
cheat

DOMINIC

THE CONTEST CONTINUED, and Dominic watched his fellow magicians, his finger running down the schedule of names. Z was so lucky. Going first meant he could sit back and enjoy the rest of the competition. Meanwhile, Dominic had to focus on keeping calm. *Breathe in, breathe out,* he told himself. *Visualize your routine and imagine you are performing without a hitch.* Ariel had insisted that imagining success was a good technique for fighting anxiety, and she was right. Little by little, Dominic relaxed. And he remained that way even when the girl before him finished her routine to wild applause. Instead of feeling intimidated, Dominic pretended everyone was clapping for him. Then the audience settled down, and the emcee called his name.

Dominic breathed in and out one more time before stepping to the front. Once at the table, he reached into his backpack and pulled out a Sharpie, a packet of large Post-its, and his copy of *Lost: Fifty True Survival Stories*.

"Hello, everyone." He looked at the audience. *They're just normal people*, he told himself.

"For my act, I'll need a volunteer," he said, scanning the crowd. Maria Elena waved her arms wildly, but he needed a stranger. If the judges learned they were related, they'd think she was a stooge. So instead of his sister, he pointed to a teenage girl sitting in the third row. "How about you?"

"Me?" she said, pointing at herself, and when he nodded, she joined him.

"Ladies and gentlemen," Dominic began. "Today I will demonstrate my psychic abilities. Right before your very eyes, I will read someone's mind. But first"—he turned to the girl—"have you ever seen me before today?"

"No," she answered.

"Have you ever talked to me on the phone or received any text messages from me?"

"I don't even know your number."

"Are you"—he paused—"my relative?"

"No."

"My classmate?"

"I'm a senior, and you're, like, in junior high."

"Are you my friend?"

"No." She shook her head for emphasis.

"Not even on Facebook?"

"Look, kiddo, we don't know each other, okay? I've never seen you or talked to you. I don't even know your name."

"There you have it," Dominic said to the audience. He was still a little nervous, but when he glanced at Ariel, she gave him a thumbs-up, which made him feel more confident. "We are total strangers, so there is no way we could have planned this trick in advance."

Everyone nodded except Stewart. He was wiping his rec specs with a handkerchief and completely ignoring the competition. Amazingly, Dominic didn't care. Stewart wasn't a judge, so what did it matter?

"Take this." Dominic handed the girl his book. "In a few seconds, I'm going to turn my back while you open the book to any page you want. You can turn to page one or seventy-two. It doesn't matter to me. When you find a page, I want you to pick a word."

"Any word?" she asked.

"Any *visual* word. Don't pick something like 'the' or 'but' or 'than.' My mind-reading powers work only with pictures, so pick something you can *see*, like an action or an object. And when you find this word, don't say it aloud. Just think it, okay?"

She nodded, so he turned his back while she opened the book and scanned a page.

"I'm ready," she said, closing the book. "I found a word."

She handed him the book, but all Dominic did was slap a giant Post-it on the cover. He gave it back to her, along with a Sharpie. "Now," he said, "the audience wants to know what you're thinking, but you can't say it aloud. So when I turn my back again, spell out the word on the Post-it, real big, and then show it to everyone, okay?"

She nodded again, and Dominic turned his back. In big letters, she wrote "fireman" on the Post-it. Then she showed it to the audience. "They know what my word is," she said.

But Dominic kept his back turned. "Before I face you,

take that Post-it, crumple it up, and throw it away so that I have no chance of peeking at your word."

She did as he asked. "Okay, you can turn around now," she said.

He did, taking the Sharpie and the book from her. He stuck another Post-it on the cover and stared at the girl, his forehead creased with concentration. In fact, he was so focused on his trick that he actually forgot other people were in the room. "I'm establishing our psychic connection," he explained. "Just keep thinking of the word. It's very difficult to read someone's mind, so this might take a while." He closed his eyes and sniffed around. "I smell something. I smell...hot dogs and...Fritos!" The audience giggled. Then he glanced at Loop. "Hey, buddy, I know you're superhungry right now, but calm down a bit. Your food fantasies are interfering with my psychic abilities." Loop gave him the "okay" signal, and Dominic turned back to the girl. "Okay, now. Focus on that word. Think only of that *one word* while I draw it on this Post-it." He held the book close to his face so no one else could see it. "I see...limbs...tree limbs?" He scribbled something. "No, wait! Limbs as in appendages as in...as in legs. But what kind of legs?" He glanced at the girl. "Keep thinking.

We're getting somewhere. I see four legs. Aha, a table per-haps." The audience giggled. "No, no, no," he said. "I see *two* legs. A ladder, there's definitely a ladder. It keeps fad-ing in and out. You have to concentrate!"

"I *am*!" the girl said.

He stared at her once again. "Yes! It's crystal clear now." He scribbled furiously, taking an exhausted breath when he finished. "My psychic powers are second to none!" he said triumphantly. "Behold!" He turned the book toward the audience so they could see the picture. Everyone cracked up.

"Dude!" a heckler said. "It's just a stick man. It could be anyone! Your psychic powers are weak!"

Dominic shrugged it off because he'd purposely messed up. Then he glanced at Z, since he was the one who sug-gested adding a magician-in-trouble phase to his routine.

Dominic looked at his Post-it again. "Hmm..." he said. "Looks like I forgot to draw this." He scribbled some-thing. "And this." He scribbled some more. "And *this*!" He examined his picture for a moment and smiled as he slowly revealed his revised drawing. "I guess a fireman needs a ladder, a hose, and a hydrant, doesn't he?"

Everyone's eyes widened with wonder. Stewart put his

rec specs back on so he could take a look, too. *It's over,* Dominic realized, *and I didn't freak out.*

He took a bow, and everyone applauded. Then he returned to his seat. Z whispered, "Way to go!" and Loop said, "You aced it!"

Dominic glanced back to see his family. He couldn't get their attention since they were giving one another high fives, but he smiled when he caught his mom and dad slapping hands.

finale—
the last part of a
performance, usually
the most exciting
moment

LOOP

LOOP WAS HAVING A great time. One guy did a chop cup routine that ended with an amazing load—a giant eyeball! Loop cracked up when the guy said, "Don't forget to keep your eye on the ball." And then a girl did a card-to-impossible-location routine. She had a spectator sign a card, did a sequence of card tricks, and in the end, took out a lemon and cut it open to reveal the signed card inside! Loop's trick required a load, too, so he paid special attention to this sleight. He used to think that knowing the secrets of magic would ruin the fun, but it wasn't true.

When you knew the secrets, you could appreciate magicians on a whole new level. It was like viewing magic from the inside looking out instead of the outside looking in.

Of course, a few kids made mistakes. They flashed or stuttered or forgot what they were doing. It was bound to happen. But most of them did a great job, including Loop's friends. Dominic and Z hadn't messed up at all, which *had* to mean that O.G. had answered Loop's petition. And that meant *he* was going to perform without messing up, too—at least that's what he believed. So he relaxed and enjoyed himself. He wasn't anxious at all. Not one tiny bit! At least, not until the emcee announced that it was Stewart's turn.

When he heard his name, Stewart went to the front, placed a red cylinder and a magic wand on the table, straightened his rec specs, and then repeated one of the most important rules of the Magician's Code. "A magician gives credit where credit is due," he said, "so I would like to acknowledge Mariano Goni's 'Nut Waltz' for inspiring this routine and Johann Strauss for writing *The Blue Danube*, which will be my musical accompaniment." He nodded to the contest director, who flipped a switch on the sound system in the back corner of the room.

As a classical waltz started to play, Stewart picked up the

wand and twirled it. Then he lifted the cylinder to reveal that a clear glass with three walnuts was hidden inside. He peeked through the cylinder like a pirate with a telescope in order to prove it was hollow, and he tapped the glass and walnuts in order to prove they were solid. He did all these actions expressively and in perfect time with the music. Then he placed the empty glass upside down and covered it with the cylinder. He did a brief French drop routine with one of the walnuts, making it disappear and reappear. Then, he closed his hand over it, waved the magic wand, and made it vanish completely. He pretended to be confused, but of course the walnut was under the glass, which was under the cylinder. And that was his routine. First, one walnut appeared under the glass and cylinder, then two walnuts, and finally three. It wasn't a complicated act, but Stewart's performance was mesmerizing. He added flourishes. He used meaningful expressions and body language. And he kept every move, even the tiniest ones, in sync with the music.

Loop was beginning to understand what Ariel meant by performance. It meant doing the moves of a magic trick without a hitch *and* doing them with style. Stewart, Loop realized, was a genius when it came to style. No other competitor had captured the audience's attention as well as he was doing right now, and he was doing it without speaking a word, which was exactly what Loop had planned!

Suddenly, Z elbowed him. "Do you have to go to the bathroom?" he asked.

That's when Loop realized his leg was shaking. Why was it shaking so much? Was he nervous? He was about to perform, and all of a sudden, he was *nervous*!

He glanced back at the audience and searched for his parents. His mom and grandma were whispering to each other during the final stages of Stewart's act, but Rubén turned to Loop, as if he could sense that Loop needed him. When they caught each other's glance, Rubén pretended to tip the baseball cap and gave Loop a wink. That small gesture said, "You got this" and "I'm here for you."

Loop thought about the book he had read over the summer. Dr. Frankenstein was like a dad. He was supposed to take care of the monster because *all* kids—even those who were not human—needed someone to make them feel safe, just like Rubén had made Loop feel safe when he winked at him. That's when Loop got the *real* message of Mr. Garza's trick, the Homing Card—because no matter how hard Loop pushed Rubén away, he'd always come back around.

Loop's thoughts were interrupted because the audience clapped. Stewart had finished his routine, which meant it was almost time for Loop's performance. He waited. A couple of minutes later, the emcee called his name. When Loop stood, he was back to his old self. He was there to have fun, so instead of walking to the front of the room, he did the moonwalk, and everybody cracked up.

The only thing his horror-film voice said before he signaled for the sound track was "Viewer discretion advised."

When the contest director pressed "play," a bunch of industrial sounds came out of the speakers—cranks, hammers, and screeching metal. *It's showtime!* Loop thought to himself as he did a few robot moves to warm up.

Then he held out his right hand and showed it to the audience, first the back of the hand and then the palm. It was empty. He made a fist, shook it a bit, and when he reopened his hand, a quarter appeared. Loop took it with his left hand, and again revealed that his right hand was empty. This time, he did a coins-across move by making two fists and pretending to toss the quarter from left to right. He even moved his eyes as if he could see an invisible quarter flying through the air. Sure enough, when he opened his hands, the coin had moved.

Now he tapped the quarter against the table and bit on it, all to prove it was solid. Then he robo-walked to a teenager in the front row, handing him the quarter and a Sharpie. Loop mimed scribbling, and the guy got the message. He wrote his initials on the coin.

Loop retrieved it and moonwalked a few steps back. Before moving on, he glanced at Mr. Garza, because the next phase was completely inspired by Señor Surprise. Loop opened his mouth and stuck out his tongue like when the doctor wants to peer down your throat. He put the quarter on his tongue and made a big show of swallowing it, nearly gagging a few times, and finally gulping loudly. Once he got the quarter down, he opened his mouth to reveal that it was empty.

After a few more dance moves, Loop started rubbing his neck with a slightly freaked-out expression on his face. He rubbed his shoulder as if it ached, and then he showed his arm to the audience. Nothing was there, but he still had this freaked-out expression. So he reached into his jeans, took out his Terror Blade, and at the moment his sound track made a slicing noise, Loop cut open his arm!

Ariel shrieked, even though she knew how the trick worked, that he wasn't really hurting himself. Loop gave her a look that said "I warned you," but inside, he was thanking her for adding to the suspense.

Some blood trickled down his arm as he put the Terror Blade away, and then he reached into his wound, making a few people cringe. He winced with pain as he dug into his arm until finally, a quarter, *the* quarter, emerged. It had traveled from his mouth, down his throat, through his shoulder and bicep, all the way to his forearm! The quarter was bloody, so he wiped it on his jeans before offering it to the teenage boy to examine.

"No way!" the guy said. "It has my initials!"

He was the first one to clap, and since that was the end of the routine, Loop bowed. The whole audience applauded, so he bowed a second time and even blew kisses at the crowd. He totally hammed it up. Who cared if the emcee was ready to take over again? Everyone was there—his family and friends—*his dad!* And Loop was having the time of his life.

finish clean—
when a magician
completes a routine and
hands the spectators his
props to prove that they
are not gimmicks

DOMINIC, LOOP AND Z

AFTER THE COMPETITION, DOMINIC, Loop, and Z sat by the pool and talked about the routines they'd seen. They went over every detail, comparing similar acts and judging who messed up and who totally aced it. Some of the kids were as good as professionals, but others were noobs. The boys knew they weren't pros, but they didn't feel like noobs, either. They guessed that they were somewhere in the middle, but that didn't stop them from wanting to win.

"Wouldn't it be cool if we got first, second, and third place?" Dominic said.

"Yeah," Loop replied, "as long as *I* get first."

"Why should *you* win?" Z asked.

"Because *my* trick's the most visual. I'm the only one who used blood, remember?"

"Well, *my* trick had more sleights," Z argued.

Dominic pointed at himself. "Don't forget about me. *I'm* the one who had the most obstacles to overcome."

"Why's that?" Z asked. "*You* didn't have to search for jobs this summer."

"Maybe not, but I *did* have severe stage fright. Talk about wanting to throw up."

"That's nothing," Loop said. "I had to learn a magic routine *and* read a superlong book with a bunch of old-fashioned words *and* draw pictures about it. Plus, my mom made me clean up my room *three* times this summer!"

Dominic and Z glanced at each other because *they* had to clean their rooms every day.

"Hi, guys." The boys turned and spotted Ariel heading toward them. "What are you talking about?"

Loop answered her question with another question. "Who do you think's going to win? Me, Dominic, or Z?"

She sat on the edge of a nearby chaise longue. "Are you serious? The contest is over, so quit arguing about who's going to win and just *relax*. How often do you get to hang out in a fancy hotel?"

"But we *need* to know," Z said. "The suspense is killing us!"

"I'm sure the judges have already made their decision," Ariel said. "Your fates are sealed." With that, she stretched out on the chaise longue, clasped her hands behind her head, and closed her eyes like someone getting a tan. "If it helps," she added, her eyes still closed, "I no longer consider you noobs. From now on, you're the Cool-Cat Conjurers in my book."

"You mean your memoir?" Z asked.

She smiled. "Exactly." Then she blinked open one eye to take a peek at them. "Besides," she added, "winning's not as great as you think."

"Why not?" Dominic said.

"Because it disqualifies you from future competitions. Trust me, I'd rather be performing than watching everybody else have all the fun." She yawned, and when a few moments passed in silence, the boys figured Ariel had fallen asleep.

"She makes a good point," Dominic said. "Next year's the stage contest. We can be like Criss Angel and do something really impressive." He thought for a second. "Maybe I can take Diamonds and Spades and turn them into tigers!"

"Quit dreaming!" Loop laughed. "Where are you going to get tigers? You're better off turning them into rabbits."

"Or iguanas," Z suggested. "It's easy to get iguanas."

"I'm not using animals in *my* routine," Loop said. "I'm doing the Zigzag Illusion. I've been dying to use a saw and cut somebody up. Either that, or I'm going to escape from a sealed tank of water that's hanging over a pit of fire."

"How are you going to get a fire on the stage without burning the whole place down?" Z asked. "You should do something simple, like levitating. That's what *I'm* going to do. Maybe I can do the dancing cane while floating in the air."

"No way!" Loop said.

"It's possible."

"Only if you don't win," Dominic reminded them. "You can't compete next year if you win. That's why I hope I come in last. I really want to try turning cats into iguanas."

"No," Z said. "*I'm* going to come in last. I don't think the people in the back rows could see my routine. I'm sure I lost points for that."

"They totally saw *my* routine," Loop said, "and they were freaked out by the blood. I saw a lady gag. So the judges probably took off points for the gross-out factor. I lost for sure."

"You're not last," Dominic said, "not when you were totally in sync with your sound track."

"Well, *you* can't come in last because you had the most audience participation." Loop looked at Z. "And *you* had the best patter."

"I did not," Z insisted. "My jokes were lame."

"At least you *had* jokes," Loop said.

"At least *you* weren't throwing up in your mouth," Dominic replied.

Ariel sat up. "Guys!" she said. "Can't a girl take a nap?" She stretched just like her cats when *they* were disturbed. "At first," she went on, "you were arguing about who's going to win and now you're arguing about who's going to lose. Does *everything* have to turn into a competition?"

The boys were silent for a while, and then they decided that, yes, life was more interesting with competitions, even silly ones. And then they invented a whole bunch of games like who was best at winning rock, paper, scissors (Loop), who was best at finding shapes in the clouds (Dominic), who was fastest at guzzling tall glasses of lemonade (Z), and who could stand longest with bare feet on the hot concrete (Ariel).

They were *still* inventing games when Ariel told them it was time to get ready for the awards ceremony. And, later, they were still debating about who'd come in first and who last when they took their seats in the auditorium, and even at the moment Ariel stepped onto the stage, opened an envelope, and announced, "The winner of this year's TAOM teen close-up contest is..."

FROM ARIEL'S NOTEBOOK

As the reigning champion of last year's TAOM teen stage contest, it was my honor to announce this year's results. Stewart was runner-up yet again. And it serves him right! He strongly implied that he'd be performing a center deal during his performance, but he didn't even use cards! Surely, he was bluffing in an attempt to throw off our composure with a cheap psych-out move.

The winner was a guy who did a classic cups-and-balls routine, much like the routine of Dai Vernon, the Professor, whose act has remained a staple of magic for more than seventy years. Perhaps my father is correct in his belief that the classic acts never go out of style, or perhaps he secretly influenced one of the judges during the convention's free breakfast for magicians formally inducted into the Order of Willard.

I will never know.

At the end of the day, however, I'm the one who remains the true winner this year, even though I did not compete. How can anyone disagree? After all, I got a prize better than a giant trophy because I won three new friends—the Cool-Cat Conjurers, AKA Dominic, Loop, and Z.

THE VAULT

Magicians never reveal their secrets, but with a little bit of research and a lot of practice, you can do any of the tricks featured in this book.

Five Books on Mr. Garza's Shelves
1. *Tarbell Course in Magic*, Volumes 1–8, by Dr. Harlan Tarbell and Ralph W. Read
2. *Card College*, Volumes 1–5, by Robert Giobbi
3. *The Dai Vernon Book of Magic* by Lewis Ganson
4. *Modern Coin Magic* by J. B. Bobo
5. *The Books of Wonder*, Volumes 1–2, by Tommy Wonder and Stephen Minch

Ten Props in Mr. Garza's Bins

1. Chop cups
2. Cups and balls
3. Decks of cards
4. Coin shells
5. Ropes
6. Sponge balls
7. Thumb tips
8. Silks
9. Gaff cards
10. Invisible thread loops

Ten Sleights Every Magician Should Learn

1. Double lift
2. Elmsley count or false count
3. Classic palm or finger palm
4. Holding a break
5. French drop
6. Crisscross force or Hindu force
7. Double undercut
8. False cut
9. False transfer of objects
10. Houdini color change

BEHIND THE MAGIC

A magician gives credit where credit is due. Here are the names of tricks performed in *Nothing Up My Sleeve*. Many are featured in books or videos online. Others are gimmicks that you can buy.

Stewart's Trick
- Nut Waltz by Mariano Goni

Ariel's Tricks
- Thread magic
- Silk Cascade
- Blooming Blossom by Mission Magic
- Dancing Cane

Mr. Garza's Tricks

- Billiard ball manipulation
- Miser's Dream by T. Nelson Downs
- Homing Card by Francis Carlyle
- Oil and Water by Juan Tamariz

Dominic's Tricks

- Hot Rod
- Die-ception by Ed Marlo
- Word in a Million by Nicholas Einhorn

Loop's Tricks

- Mafia Manicure by Giovanni Livera
- Coins Across by Jonathan Townsend
- Sick by Sean Fields

Z's Tricks

- Pen-through-Dollar
- Cut-and-Restored Rope
- Ambitious Card
- Ultimate Ambition by Daryl "the Magician's Magician"

ACKNOWLEDGMENTS

A big thank-you to Stefanie von Borstel at Full Circle Literary for being my agent and friend. Also thanks to the wonderful editors, Alvina Ling and Allison Moore, whose suggestions and insights did much to help me improve this novel, and to the entire team at Little, Brown for their encouragement and support.

I want to give a special acknowledgment to my nephews, the Martinez boys—Steban, Seth, Deven, and Zachary. They are the ones who asked me to write a book for boys and who answered the call when I needed help with dialogue or scenes. They have also brought much love and joy to my life.

Finally, my inspiration for this book comes from the

fact that I know too much about magic but cannot perform any tricks. This is because of my magician friends. Here's a shout-out to Rolando Medina, Mike Cruz (AKA Spikey Mikey), and Julio Ramirez, owner of JCR Magic, the shop that inspired Conjuring Cats. The biggest shout-out, however, goes to my husband, Gene, who generously shared all his magic know-how and extensive collection of props, books, and lecture notes. He also let me tag along at magic lectures and, of course, the annual TAOM Convention, where I got the idea for an amateur close-up contest. Thanks, Gene, for helping me brainstorm, for reading my drafts, and for being my best friend!